Sir Tristan of All Time

Sir Tristan of All Time
by Sabra Holbrook

Farrar, Straus & Giroux New York

AN ARIEL BOOK

Lines from "Tristan's Singing," in *Poems* by John Masefield, have been reprinted with the permission of The Macmillan Company. Copyright 1931 by John Masefield, renewed 1959 by John Masefield.

Lines from *The Famous Tragedy of the Queen of Cornwall* by Thomas Hardy have been reprinted with the permission of the Estate of Thomas Hardy, Macmillan & Co. Ltd., London, The Macmillan Company of Canada Limited, and The Macmillan Company, New York. Copyright 1925 by The Macmillan Company.

Lines from "Tristram," in *Collected Poems* by Edwin Arlington Robinson, have been reprinted with the permission of The Macmillan Company. Copyright 1927 by Edwin Arlington Robinson, renewed 1955 by Ruth Nivison and Barbara R. Holt.

≋ FOR

Marie H. LeLavandier
my Vassar Professor of Medieval French
in affectionate memory

———————————

Contents

ACKNOWLEDGMENTS

The author is grateful to Mr. Albert G. Craz, Chairman of the English Department of School District No. 2, Syosset, New York, for reviewing the manuscript of this book and making many valuable suggestions. For detailed information on Castle Dor, the author is indebted to field research undertaken by Mrs. Jean Batham and Miss Isabel Beckett. For access to the Palais de Justice and the Maubergeon Tower in Poitiers, France, she thanks Madame Laillard of the Poitiers Syndicat d'Initiative. For arrangements to visit the birthplace and church built by Eleanor of Aquitaine, she is grateful for arrangements made for her by Monsieur Leroy of the Commissariat Général au Tourisme in Bordeaux, as well as for the assistance and explanations provided by the Mayor of Belin.

The research for this book—though not with the book in mind—commenced when the author was a student at Vassar College; was intermittently carried on, partly in England, France, and Germany, and was recently renewed for the purpose of presenting Tristan to modern young Americans. To the many friends and scholars who over this period of time have contributed to the author's concern with the subject, she is continuously in debt.

Part I

THE LEGEND

Bele amie, si est de nus:
Ne vus sanz mei, ne jo sanz vus.

Here is the crux of our two lives:
Without the other, neither thrives.

From Le Lai du Chevrefeuille *(Honeysuckle*
Song), being the account of Tristan and Iseut
given by Marie de France in 1230

Sir Tristan
of Twelfth-Century France

*Turn the calendar back eight hundred years and come
to a university in Western Europe. Most of the students*
are teen-agers, for, in the century to which your calendar lies open, university life can begin at thirteen. Like
young people of all times and places, these teen-agers are
questioning the patterns into which adults expect them
to fit. They question especially the established professions for which they are being trained: clergy or clerking, teaching or law.

As twelfth-century teen-agers see their world, there is
a more exciting way to get the most out of life. That

way is to become a romance-weaver-in-residence at the court of some highborn lord or lady. In such a court, bed, board, and revelry are free—not to mention the handsome wages. Court life may be risky, depending on noble whim, but never is it dull. To the students the prospect glitters, in contrast with grubbing over Latin declensions and ancient literature, then—if they pass a stiff final examination—graduating into underling positions that require still more grubbing.

In the twelfth century there was tremendous demand for court entertainers with gifted pens and glib tongues. Especially in France, the arts of writing and reciting flourished, reaching their most polished form in the *romans courtois*—romantic tales spun for the delight of royalty. The love legend of Sir Tristan and his Iseut is one of these tales, the only one so powerful that through all the ages, down to our time, artists, musicians, and writers have continued to use it as a basis for new masterpieces.

The first versions, mostly in verse, were set down between seven hundred and eight hundred years ago by different storytellers in England, France, and Germany. Some of the authors' names have survived; others have been forgotten. Some were university students or recent graduates, close to the age of the lovers whose story they told. Tristan and Iseut, too, were teen-agers.

The universities from which these Tristan chroniclers came were quite different from any today. A *Universi-*

tas (the Latin name for university) was merely a corpo-
ration, formed by professors, sometimes with the help of
would-be students. The corporations, the first colleges
of Western civilization, were a collection of people
rather than of buildings. In rented classrooms professors
stood and students sat on the floor. Particularly in
northern France, bevies of such corporations were
founded in the early 1100's. Students flocked to them,
not only from France but from all Europe.

Despite the informality of atmosphere, the subject
matter in the universities was rigid: Latin literature,
logic, philosophy, religious law and doctrine, astronomy,
and mathematics. There were also courses in expressive
writing and speech, which were a help to students who
had their hearts set on becoming entertainers to nobility.
By making friends with classmates of noble birth, bud-
ding writers could open doors to the future employment
of their dreams. In the course of a hundred years, student ferment and changing times forced the universities to offer a greater range of studies more related to the
real world, but during the century of change, many a
student with a lively imagination chafed.

One such imaginative student is believed to have been
Chrétien de Troyes, who in 1165 was one of the earliest
recorders of the Tristan love story. It is not hard to vis-
ualize him, sitting cross-legged on the moldering straw
scattered on his classroom floor, only half listening to his

professor's lecture on logic, while dreaming of the spell his verses might create in castle halls. One professor of Chrétien's day, struggling with the likes of him, wrote to an associate: "I believe the devil is in these poets!"

After Chrétien graduated, he traveled in England. Perhaps he had made a connection in school with the son of a noble English family. Englishmen of the time were eager to engage French poets and paid them generously. Probably while in England, Chrétien picked up a story, already going the rounds there, of an eighth-century tribal ruler in Scotland. He and others clothed this historical figure with their own imagination and transformed him into Sir Tristan, a brave and handsome knight of their own time, the late Middle Ages.

According to the legend, first built around the tribesman, afterward transferred to English and French nobility, and then embellished by at least eight twelfth- and thirteenth-century writers, the love of Tristan and his lady, Iseut, was so powerful that not even death could defeat it. In fact, the couple became immortal in ways the "devil-poets" could not have foreseen. Iseut the Golden-Haired, whose beauty caused crowds to stare wherever she went, and Tristan, the lover who dared all for her, have intrigued other poets through the ages. They have inspired not only poetry but also novels, drama, music, and art. They are of our time, yet still of their time, of times between and of times to come.

Shall we meet them in Chrétien's time?

The year is 1170. The place is Poitiers, France, in the castle of Eleanor of Aquitaine, Duchess of Poitou and Normandy, Countess of Anjou, Queen of England and a former Queen of France. On long leave from her lord, the King of England, with whom she is quarreling, she presides over the Poitiers court, headquarters of territory inherited from her father. Presiding with her is her daughter, Countess Marie de Champagne, a princess of France and patron of Chrétien de Troyes.

Chrétien was one of several poets employed in Eleanor's hilltop castle at Poitiers, and it might have been he who on this night was selected to entertain the assembled nobles with the reading of the Tristan and Iseut romance, which he had set in rhyme some five years before. Or it might have been a visiting English poet of French ancestry, Thomas, who had also written a Tristan poem. Or perhaps it was a frequent Welsh guest in French courts, Breri, who recited his even older version. Researchers, who have worked like detectives to solve the mystery that still surrounds the Tristan legend and its authors, claim that Breri and Thomas were welcomed in Poitiers, where the Tristan story was a favorite.

Whoever the narrator, he takes his stand in the center of a great, oblong hall with a three-story-high vaulted ceiling. Seated on stone benches under arcades around the sides, the noblemen wait, idly stirring with their pointed shoes the sweet-smelling rushes freshly strewn upon the floor. Through arched windows behind them, a

view of terraces planted with chestnut trees spreads out,
and beyond and below, the valley of the Vienne River
fades from twilight blue to darkness and is lost from
sight. Inside, servants light tapers. An orchestra of ten
or more musicians assembles on a lofty balcony, elabo-
rately railed with grilled iron, at the far end of the hall.
Below the balcony, three huge fireplaces, piled with pine
logs, serve for heat in winter. The orchestra strikes up.
They are playing lutes, forerunners of the guitar; viols
and rotes, primitive forms of the violin; zither-like dul-
cimers and harps. Other nobles arrive during this overture. Their long, silken garments with flowing sleeves
are fur-trimmed and slashed to let brilliant-colored lin-
ings show through. Their cloaks boast embroidered borders. The younger men wear their hair long.

The ladies of the court seat themselves on a dais at the
opposite end of the hall from the musicians. They too
are richly dressed, their softly pleated, floor-length
gowns belted with gold and jewels at the waist. Their
heads are coiffed with flowing veils, and flowing trains
trail from their shoulders, rustling through the rushes as
they walk.

Queen Eleanor sits in the center of the group, her
daughter on her right. The Queen nods to the narrator.
He holds up his hand, on which a topaz ring, the gift of
a patron, gleams in the candlelight. The orchestra is
quiet. One musician plucks the strings of his harp in a
rippling chord, and the narrator begins:

"My lords and ladies: Would it please you to listen to a noble tale of love and death? It is the tale of Tristan and of Iseut, the Queen. Hear how, in great joy and great grief, they loved one another, and at last both died of love on the same day, lying side by side."

Quickly the narrator sketches the background of the story. He explains that the hero was the son of Rivalen, King of the fabled land of Lyonesse, and Blanchefleur, sister of Marc, King of Cornwall in England. Rivalen was killed in battle against Morgan, an enemy baron. Shortly afterward his child was born to Blanchefleur, and grieving for her husband, she named the infant Tristan, from *triste*, the French word for sad.

"She named him, she kissed him, and she died." The narrator sighs, pauses, and plunges into his tale.

"Morgan, the enemy, drew near to the castle gates. Rohalt, the Faith-Keeper, a trusted liege of Rivalen, feared for the princeling's life. He fled with Tristan and, keeping secret the child's royal heritage, reared him as his son.

"The lad grew comely, tall and lean, broad of shoulder. He learned all knightly skills: to wield the lance and sword and bear the shield—fully armed to ride his horse as though he and steed were one. He learned to leap with a single bound the widest castle moat, to hunt with bow and arrow. He minded well the code of knighthood: to keep his promises, rescue the weak, and scorn all lies and evildoing.

"Then, one day, traders who had sailed from Norway lured Tristan to their ship and made off with him as booty. But it is proven, and every mariner knows, that the sea hates ships of evilhearted men. Furiously the waves rose, surrounding the vessel on every side. For eight days and eight nights the ship was battered and the traders quaked. Then on the ninth day they saw ahead the coast of Cornwall, bristling with jagged rocks and cliffs. In terror of more vengeance, they set the boy ashore—and in that moment the sea calmed.

"Tristan scaled a steep cliff to a forest on its crest. There he met a band of hunters and offered them his help in the chase. The huntsmen were astonished at his skill, so much greater than their own.

" 'Friend,' said the master of the chase, 'where did you learn your artful ways? Tell us your country and your name.'

" 'Sir, I am called Tristan of Lyonesse, and if you wish I will join your band and teach you all I know.'

" 'Be welcome among us, Tristan. We shall take you to King Marc, our noble lord, in the castle of Tintagel.'

"Now when the hunters brought Tristan to Marc, the King looked upon the lad and could not turn his eyes away. Affection overwhelmed him. 'From where does this warm feeling come?' the King asked of his heart, and his heart made no reply.

"My good lords and ladies, it was the King's blood which talked to him from his veins. It was the love with which he had cherished his sister, Tristan's mother, Blanchefleur. And so uncle and nephew met, neither knowing they were of one blood.

"My lords and ladies, the teller of tales who would please you must not talk forever. This tale contains so much of beauty as it is—why should I stretch it out? In brief, Tristan became the liege of Marc and by him was made a knight, and great love grew between them. Then after three years Rohalt, searching for Tristan, found him in Cornwall. He told Marc who the young knight truly was; likewise he told Tristan himself. And Tristan returned with Rohalt to Lyonesse and did battle with the baron Morgan who had slain his father and taken his lands. When he had killed the enemy and thus avenged the wrong, he gave his heritage to Rohalt and returned to Marc."

The storyteller pauses while the harp plays an interlude. No one in the audience stirs. Knowing that he holds the interest of all, the narrator continues:

"When Tristan returned, he found all Cornwall in deep gloom. The King of Ireland had equipped a fleet and threatened to ravage the country unless Marc sent him forthwith three hundred fifteen-year-old boys and three hundred fifteen-year-old girls. These youths of noble birth were destined to a life as slaves.

"To proclaim his terms, the Irish King had sent to Cornwall Morholt, the giant, in a ship with purple sails. Marc and his barons assembled to hear the giant speak.

One hope Morholt held out. If any baron would do battle with him, why then, should the baron win, the children need not go.

"The barons with bowed heads looked secretly at each other. 'Have we brought you up, dear sons, to carry the burdens of slaves, and you, dear daughters, to become the playthings of lewd men?' So said they to themselves. 'But our dying would not save you and the giant would surely kill us.' And no one spoke aloud.

"Then Tristan knelt at Marc's feet and spoke. 'My lord, the King, if it please you to award me this honor, I will do battle with the giant.'

"Marc could not dissuade him. Morholt and Tristan sailed to an islet off the coast. The barons waited on the ramparts of Tintagel. They could not see the duel on the islet, but they could hear, even from afar, the fierce ring of steel on steel as swords crossed and clashed.

"In the late day, a ship with purple sails set toward the shore. 'The Morholt!' the barons groaned. But as the vessel neared, they saw Tristan astride its prow, a sword in either hand. Blood gushing from his wounds, he sailed the ship, brandishing his sword and the sword of the giant he had slain.

"Twenty boats plied out to meet him and the boys and girls of Cornwall threw themselves into the surf and swam to where he was. Their mothers knelt on the beach and kissed his feet as he landed. Bells pealed, horns and trumpets sounded with such a din no man could have heard God had he thundered.

"But though Tristan had freed the people, he himself was mortally wounded by the poisoned sword of Morholt. Day by day, he drew nearer to death. At last he begged the King to lay him in a small boat and give him his harp and set him adrift at sea.

" 'Perhaps,' he said, 'the waves will bear me where I may find someone to heal me of my grievous wounds. Then will I return to serve you as your liege.'

"For seven days and seven nights the sea rocked him gently onward, and on the seventh night some fishermen heard a faint melody across the waves. In the first whiteness of the dawn, they saw the wandering boat. They rowed aside it and found Tristan, his hands fresh fallen from his harp. They bore him to one who, of her mercy and her skill, might heal him.

"That one was Iseut the Golden-Haired, daughter of the King of Ireland and niece of the slain Morholt. She and her mother, the Queen, knew many magic balms and potions, made from herbs picked at propitious hours, and with these Iseut healed, all unknowing, the slayer of her uncle.

"Tristan said nothing of who he was, and when he was well, left secretly lest he be recognized. And after many days he came home to Cornwall. The King was overjoyed but his jealous barons were not. 'He is a sorcerer, this man Tristan,' they said. 'How else could he have killed the giant? How else recover from a poisonous wound?'

"Marc so loved his nephew that he wished to make him his heir, but the jealous barons would not have this plan. They threatened to revolt unless Marc sought a bride. As a ruse, the King declared there was but one lady in the world he wished for queen. A swallow had brought to his windowsill a strand of golden hair, finer than silk, gleaming like a ray of sun. She to whom the hair belonged—that beauty alone would he marry.

"Tristan looked at the shining strand and smiled. He remembered Iseut the Golden-Haired, who had healed him. And though he knew what peril waited in Ireland for the slayer of Morholt, once again he risked his life for his King and set sail in quest of Iseut.

"When he came to Ireland, he found the people at the mercy of a dragon who ate young girls, crunching them faster than one could say the Lord's Prayer. The fearsome beast vomited fire through his nose; his eyes glowed like fiery coals beneath his horns. His body, with the tail of a serpent, was crusted with scales; his claws were like a lion's. To any man who could rid Ireland of this scourge, the King had promised his daughter, Iseut the Golden-Haired. Twenty valiant knights had perished in the hope of winning her.

"My lords and ladies, hope thrives on sparse pasture in the hearts of men, and with a hopeful heart Sir Tristan sought the dragon. His good sword could not pierce the scales; his horse dropped dead of poisonous fumes, his armor was blackened by the breath of fire. But when the dragon opened wide his jaws to swallow his opponent, Tristan rammed his sword down the monster's throat—and with a horrible cry, the dragon died.

"So Tristan claimed Iseut, and though the King of Ireland hated him for the death of Morholt, the King was honor-bound to keep his vow: to the dragon's slayer should go his daughter's hand. And he put Iseut's right hand in the right hand of Tristan, and Tristan clasped it in the name of the King of Cornwall.

"Iseut shook with anguish to become the captive of her uncle's slayer and to think of being led to the land where he had died. But her mother, the Queen, knew that what must be must be. At parting time, the Queen gave Iseut's lady-in-waiting, Brangien, a powerful potion made from flowers, herbs, and roots, all brewed in wine.

"She said: 'Accompany Iseut to Cornwall and be faithful. Take with you this brew and remember my words. On the wedding night, present a gobletful to Iseut and the King. Take care that they alone drink from the goblet. Guard the potion well, for this is its magic: those who drink of it together will love each other with all their hearts and all their minds, forever, in life and in death.'

"And Brangien promised to do the Queen's will.

"Now one hot day aboard the ship, when the winds had fallen and the sails hung slack, Tristan and Iseut, languishing with thirst, called for water. A young maidservant who went to fetch it found the potion. 'Look, I have found wine!' she cried. Iseut drank deeply; then, from courtesy, held the flagon out to Tristan, who emptied it.

"It seemed to Tristan that spiked thorns, but with a flowery fragrance, pushed roots into his heart's blood, from which sprang a bond that drew his flesh, his every thought, his every desire to the fair body of Iseut the Golden-Haired.

"It seemed to Iseut that a tenderness sharper than her hatred of her uncle's slayer wounded her heart. She put her arm on Tristan's shoulder; her eyes clouded with tears; her lips trembled.

" 'Dear friend, what is it that torments you?' Tristan asked, and she replied: 'The love of you.' Then he put his lips on hers. And when the evening came they gave themselves up wholly to their love. The wind rose and the ship heeled and ever more rapidly it carried them to Cornwall.

"Upon the shore Marc welcomed them and escorted Iseut to Tintagel. When she entered the dusky great hall where the barons were assembled, her beauty, shining forth, lighted the very walls, as though with the glow of the rising sun. And Marc gave thanks for the swallow who had brought him a strand of her hair, and praised Tristan, who had brought her to him."

The narrator interrupts his tale. "Alas, O noble King," he warns, as if Marc sat in his audience, "what harsh torments have also sailed to you aboard the ship that bore your Queen."

The harp ripples a deep, ominous chord, like faraway thunder. The narrator continues:

"In eighteen days Marc wed Iseut in the presence of his court. On the wedding night, when the King's chamber was dark, Brangien slipped into Marc's bed and he did not know her from the Queen. Thus did Brangien sacrifice her purity to save her lady from shame and death—for, as the custom was, Marc would have killed Iseut had he known she was not wholly his.

"Now Brangien had told the lovers of the potion's power and they knew of what deadly magic they had drunk. They knew why love pressed them harder every day, as thirst presses a stag to the stream or hunger plummets a hawk to its prey. And Tristan's heart was torn between the love of Iseut and the love of Marc. But how could he challenge fate? 'It is not dishonor that I do,' he reasoned, 'nor shame I bring upon my uncle and my lord, the King, for I am prisoner of the potion, and God, the King of the world, who sees all, will defend us.'

"In the manner of the court, Tristan, a noble knight, was always close to the Queen and slept with other

faithful nobles in the royal chambers. While Brangien
kept watch, the lovers were together. Never were they
found in each other's arms, but on their faces was not
their passion, working like new wine, plain for every
man to see?

"And jealous barons saw it. Among them were four
villains whose names I can recount—Andret, Guenelon,
Gondoine, and Denoalen—and may God curse their
souls. They went to the King and said: 'Good King,
your heart will no doubt be troubled by our news and
we also mourn, but you must hear that Tristan loves the
Queen. It is a proven fact and already people babble of
it.'

"The King staggered as if struck. He called the
barons cowards and sent them off. But he could not put
from his mind the poison they had planted. He called
Tristan to him and told him what they had said. 'I do
not believe them, but their evil words have troubled my
heart,' he confessed. 'It will be quieted only if you leave
us for a while. Leave, my dear nephew, whom I call my
son. Leave and no doubt I will recall you soon.'

"But Tristan could not leave. He hid in a peasant's
house and Brangien found a way for the lovers to keep
tryst. Never, my lords and ladies, have you heard tell of
a more artful deception. Behind the castle of Tintagel
stretched an orchard, fenced high with pointed stakes.

At the far end of the orchard stood a tall, straight pine, with wide and drooping branches. At the foot of the tree a lively spring welled into a clear, calm pool, set in marble. From the pool the water spilled into a stream that flowed through the orchard and into the castle.

"As Brangien advised, Tristan leaped the fence each night and, cutting bits of bark and twigs from the pine, dropped them into the stream. Light as foam, they floated to Iseut, waiting within the castle walls. Seeing them, she knew that Tristan waited too. And on such nights as Brangien could devise distraction for the King, Iseut came to her lover. And the darkness and the friendly shadow of the great pine tree protected them.

" 'Tristan,' said Iseut one night when the dark was fading, 'do not magicians say Tintagel is enchanted and that twice a year, in winter and again in summer, some spell banishes it from men's sight? This is the time. It has vanished now, and here are we in the heavenly orchard of which harpists sing. A wall of air encloses us on all sides. Here a hero may live forever in the arms of the woman he loves and no enemy may enter.'

"Already as she spoke, trumpets sounded from the towers of Tintagel, announcing the dawn. The returning light silhouetted the summits in red, then azure.

" 'No,' replied Tristan, 'this is not the time, nor this the orchard. The wall of air is already pierced. But one day, my love, we will journey together to a fortunate country from which no one returns. There stands a castle of white marble, a candle burns in each of its thousand windows; at each window a minstrel forever sings. There the sun never shines and no one misses its light.'

"Though all too short were such meetings of the lovers, Iseut recovered the joy that had left her when Tristan had been sent from court. And Andret, Guenelon, Gondoine, and Denoalen, watching her, suspected that Tristan was near. 'Let us consult Frocin, the hunchbacked dwarf,' said Andret to the others. 'He can read the stars and by their powers discover secrets. He can tell us what deception Iseut may now employ.'

"The misshapen little evil one, who hated all beauty and all happiness, studied for the barons the behavior of Orion and Lucifer. Finally he said: 'Be glad, my lords. Tonight you can seize the lovers.' The barons took him to the King.

"Against his heart's warning, the King agreed to follow the dwarf that night into the orchard. Frocin led him to the pine tree and bade him climb therein, carrying his bow and arrow. 'Be gone, dog of the enemy,' said Marc. But he climbed the tree.

"The moon shone bright. Soon, from his perch in the pine boughs, the King saw his nephew leap the fence, come to the tree, and throw the bark and twigs into the pool. As Tristan leaned over the moonlit water, he saw the reflection of the King above. He reached to stop the floating bits—but too late! They swirled rapidly from the orchard.

"Oh God, protect the lovers." The narrator clasps his hands as he continues.

"Iseut ran out from the castle. Tristan heard the King fit an arrow to his bow.

" 'What is wrong?' thought Iseut, slowing her pace. 'Tristan does not run to meet me as is his custom.' She stopped, trying to see into the night. There was nothing. Then, as she approached the pool, she too saw the reflection of the King. 'My Lord God,' she whispered to herself, 'grant to me only that I may speak first.'

" 'Sir Tristan,' she said quickly, 'why have you dared to call me to such a place at such an hour? What do you want of me? I have come because I owe you much. You brought me here to reign, a Queen. So here am I, your debtor. What would you of me?'

"Tristan praised God, who had revealed to Iseut the peril in which they stood. 'My Queen,' he answered, 'I have called you to beg you of your mercy to intervene with the King for me. He hates me and I know not why. Surely by now the fears with which Andret and those others disquieted his soul are laid to rest. Yet he is still angry. Who better can quiet his anger than you, pure and gracious Queen, in whom he puts his heart's trust?'

" 'In truth, Sir Tristan, do you not know that he suspects me too? My God knows—and if I lie, may He disgrace me bodily—that I have given my love only to the man who first took me, a maiden, in his arms. Yet my King believes I love you with a guilty love. Did he even know that I am here beneath this pine tonight—tomorrow he would have me burned, my ashes thrown to the winds. I am alone on earth, alone in this palace where no one cares for me. I am without support—at the mercy of the King. If I say to him a single word for you, I risk a shameful death. Friend, may God protect you. The King hates you most unjustly. But wherever you may go, believe this: God will be your true friend.'

"Iseut fled to the castle and when she told Brangien of her narrow escape, Brangien exclaimed: 'Iseut, my lady, God has wrought a miracle for you. He is a compassionate father and does not wish harm for the innocent.'

"Alone under the pine tree, Tristan lamented: 'May God have pity on me and undo the great injustice which I suffer from my dear King.'

"And in the branches above, Marc's conscience ached. The next day he called Tristan back to court. Andret, Guenelon, Gondoine, and Denoalen threatened to make war on him if Tristan remained. They swore the dwarf, Frocin, could still prove that Tristan was the lover of the Queen.

"And once more Marc agreed to listen to the dwarf. That night Frocin strewed flour on the floor between the bed of Tristan, near the King's bed, and the place across the chamber where Iseut lay. But Tristan saw the flour and vaulted over it, leaving no footprints. On the castle ramparts, Frocin, reading the stars, knew the lovers were together and called the King. Tristan had regained his bed and lay feigning sleep. But alas! The day before, while he was hunting in the forest, a wild boar had wounded his leg. This night, in the effort of leaping, the wound had burst open, blood gushing to the floor.

"By the light of the dwarf's lantern, the King saw the flour drenched with blood. And the four barons, who were with him, held Tristan down upon his bed and bared the wound, still dripping.

" 'Tristan,' said the King, 'no lies will help you. Tomorrow you die, and Iseut with you.'

"With lights and loud voices the castle was aroused. From guard to guard and through the black of night the news traveled to the town. Rich merchants and common men all wept, for they remembered how Tristan had rescued them from Morholt.

"At six the next morning, the King sent a messenger through the countryside, summoning the people to the castle yard. When they were assembled, he addressed them: 'Lords and citizens, I have built here, as you see, a pyre of thornbushes, where Tristan and the Queen shall burn because they have been false to honor.'

"But the crowd cried loudly: 'A trial, O King, a trial first. To kill without a trial is a shameful crime.'

"Angrily the King replied, 'No, no trial! By the God who made this world, if one more person asks me such a thing, he will be the first to burn in that furnace.' And the people were frightened and fell silent.

"Now guards had been sent to bring thither Tristan and the Queen. My noble lords and ladies, hear how the good Lord God is full of pity. He, who does not wish the death of sinners, hearkened to the tears and prayers of Marc's people as they besought His aid for the tortured lovers.

"As Tristan, unarmed and bound, was being led to the pyre, a faithful follower rode up and cut his bonds. 'It is not meet to lead him so,' he told the pair of guards. 'Should he try to escape, you have your swords.' The follower was of noble birth, owning much land, and the guards did not dare cross his will. So Tristan walked, untied, between them. And as they walked they passed a chapel on a cliff above the sea. 'Sirs,' said Tristan, 'permit me to enter that chapel. My death is near. I will pray God for mercy. The chapel has no door but this one; each of you has a sword. Well you know that I could not escape, excepting through this door. I must come out as I went in.'

"The guards let him enter. He ran the length of the chapel, leaped over the choir stalls to a stained-glass window behind the altar, forced the window open, and threw himself over the cliff. Better that end than death upon the thorn-pyre before the multitude.

"Outside the chapel, the guards waited vainly, for it was God who was now Tristan's guard. The wind lifted his cloak and dropped him gently on a large rock at the bottom of the cliff. To this day, the people of Cornwall call that rock 'Tristan's Leap.'

"Now it happened that on the shore below was Gorvenal, Tristan's servant. Fearing the King would burn him too, Gorvenal had fled, bearing Tristan's sword and helmet. He gave these to his master, thanking God.

" 'Yes, God has blessed me with his mercy,' Tristan said, 'but they will kill Iseut. Now that I am free, I must deliver her.'

" 'Do not be so hasty,' Gorvenal advised him. 'It is beyond even your prowess to approach that pyre. It is well said that foolishness is not bravery. Let us take cover in these woods nearby. Many people pass here. We will learn from them what happens, and if the King burns Iseut, I swear never to sleep until the day I have avenged her with you.' And they hid in the forest called Morois.

"Before the lighted pyre, Iseut stood erect. Tears flowed down her face. The crowd around her cried: 'Cursèd be the King, cursèd be his treacherous barons.'

"The Queen was clothed in a simple smock of gray cloth woven here and there with a thread of gold. A thread of gold was twined into her golden hair, which fell about her to her feet. Who could look upon her

beauty pitiless? That man would have the heart of a vil-
lain. Good God, how tightly were her fair arms bound!
The blood dripped from the cords.

"Just then one hundred lepers, their flesh gnawed and
bleached by their disease, hobbled on crutches to the
fire, clacking the rattles which warned all healthy souls
to keep their distance. From underneath the lepers'
swollen eyelids, their bloodshot eyes savored the
spectacle.

"The ugliest of the lepers cried to the King: 'Your
Majesty, you would throw your wife to the furnace.
This is high justice, but all too brief. That great fire will
soon burn her up. This wind will soon scatter her ashes.
Would you that I show you a worse punishment, under
which she will live always longing for death? Would
you, Your Majesty?'

"And the King replied: 'I would be the willing pupil
of the man who could teach me such a torture.'

" 'Give us Iseut,' said the leper, 'and we will share her.
When she enters our wretched hovels and lies in our
beds, when she is deformed like us, then Iseut the beautiful, Iseut the Golden-Haired, will regret her sin and
long for this splendid fire.'

" 'In mercy, Your Majesty, burn me rather!' cried
Iseut.

"The King answered her no word, but gave her to
the leper, and the other lepers pressed close, yelping with
joy. Dragging her from the town, the hideous retinue

passed the woods where Tristan and Gorvenal lay waiting. This was their chance! They rescued her from the
lepers, though Tristan, in pity for the wretched beings,
would not draw his sword against them.

"Then, carrying Iseut in his arms, Tristan fled far
into the forest, and Gorvenal with them. In its depths
they felt as safe as behind the stoutest castle walls. No
evil baron dared come in, for fear that Tristan would
hang him from the nearest tree.

"The winter came. The lovers crouched in a crevice
of rock and the frost garnished their bed of dried leaves.
They ate only the deer which Tristan shot with a willow
bow and arrows he had fashioned. He called the bow
'Never-fail,' for its aim was always true. They warmed
themselves and cooked on fagot fires which Gorvenal
stacked for them. But the faces of the lovers grew thin
and wan. Their clothes, torn by brambles, fell to rags.
'We have lost the world and the world has lost us. How
does it seem to you, Tristan, my dear one?' asked Iseut.

" 'My friend, when I have you, what else do I need?'
Tristan replied. They loved each other and they did not
suffer.

"When spring came, Tristan built a hut of leafy
branches. As a child in Lyonesse, he had learned the
songs of birds and within the hut he sang like a thrush, a
blackbird, and a nightingale. And the birds flew to an-
swer him, roosting in the hut's branches and warbling
with full throats.

"Now one day Tristan and Iseut heard the baying of a dog. Tristan knew the voice; it was his hunting greyhound, Husdent. Was the King pursuing them at last and using Husdent to track them down? They hid in a thicket. When the baying came close, Tristan stood, his bow taut. The dog bounded to him, barking with joy, and Tristan had no heart to let the arrow fly. 'What shall I do?' he asked of Iseut. 'Counsel me. Husdent will surely betray us by his barking.'

"Iseut answered. 'I have heard of a Welsh forester who trained his hound to hunt in silence. What joy, dear Tristan, if you could train Husdent.' Husdent licked her hands.

" 'I will try,' said Tristan. 'It is too hard for me to kill my dog.'

"Now, after Tristan had escaped from the chapel, Husdent had been chained in a dungeon at Tintagel. But his fierce and lonely baying, day and night, disturbed the castle from dungeon to turrets and Marc was forced to let the animal go free. The dog picked up his master's scent, sped to the chapel, sprang through the window, landed below, rolled over, shook, and headed for the forest. He had come alone. No man dared follow him to the end.

"In thirty days, with patient, daily lessons, Tristan taught Husdent to be a silent dog. In silence, they hunted together. And Husdent and the lovers and the faithful Gorvenal lived in the forest at peace.

"Now on another day, as Tristan and Iseut walked among the trees, they met a holy man, the hermit Ogrin. He called upon the lovers to repent. 'God pardons the sinner who repents,' he said.

" 'Repent?' Tristan was scornful. 'Repent of what sin? You who would judge us, do you know what draught we drank upon the sea?'

" 'Sir Tristan,' said the hermit, 'it is a mortal sin to betray your King. Return the Queen to the man with whom she was united in holy wedlock.'

" 'She is no longer his, good hermit. He gave her to the lepers and from them I rescued her. From that day forth, the Queen was mine. I cannot leave her, nor she me. Come away, Iseut.' He took her by both hands and they walked on. The trees closed their branches around them and they faded from sight in the foliage.

"Often on the leafy forest floor the two lay close, but one sultry summer afternoon, when Tristan had returned from hunting too tired and hot for love, he said, 'I will lie down and sleep a while.' Iseut lay apart from him and he placed his sword between them. While the lovers napped, a woodcutter came upon them and ran straight for Tintagel to tell the King that he had seen them.

" 'I will have vengeance,' Marc said, when the woodsman had gasped out his story. 'I will either kill those two or else be killed myself.' He bade the man lead him to the spot.

"But when they reached it and Marc saw the lovers sleeping still, with the sword between their bodies, he was astounded. 'My God,' he said, 'if indeed they love each other madly, why do they sleep thus, with a sword between them? Does not everyone know that the sword between man and woman is the guarantee and guardian of purity? It would be a sin to kill them. But I will leave a sign so they will know that I have found them and that I did not wish their death.'

"Through a chink in the branches above the couple's heads a ray of sun burned Iseut's white face. Marc took off ermine gloves which Iseut had brought him from Ireland and stuffed them in the chink. He took from Iseut's hand the ring of emeralds he had given her. Once the ring had been too tight; now it slipped too easily from her thin finger. In its place, the King put on her hand a ring Iseut had given him. Then he took the sword—the same, he recognized it, that had slayed Morholt—and laid his own sword down instead. After he had done these things, he stole away.

"When Iseut woke, she saw the gloves and ring and cried: 'Woe upon us, for the King has found us.'

"Tristan jumped from his sleep, reaching for his sword. He saw the sword was Marc's. 'He has gone to seek reinforcements. He will return,' said Tristan. 'He will burn us. Come, we must flee.'

"And, with Governal, they fled to the end of the forest where it bordered the land of Wales.

"After three days there, Tristan, caught by nightfall as he chased a deer, pondered in the dusk. Thus he thought: the King did not need to go for reinforcements. He could have killed me while I slept. From tenderness and pity, he forbore. Death by fire, death in the chapel leap, death among the lepers—from all these God saved us and the King has recognized that we are in God's keeping. Now he remembers me as the boy who gave up my kingdom for him and who shed my blood in the battle with Morholt. And Iseut? She was a Queen in his castle. In these woods she lives like a peasant. What have I done to her? Instead of rooms draped with silk, I have given her this savage forest. Ah, my Lord God, King of the World, give me the strength to return Iseut to Marc.' Tristan leaned on his bow and long he lamented in the night.

"Iseut waited for Tristan. By the light of the moon, she saw on her finger the golden circlet that Marc had slipped there. She thought: 'He who gave me this ring is not the same angry man who gave me to the lepers. No, he is again the compassionate lord who from the day when I landed in his kingdom welcomed and protected me. How he loved Tristan, and what have I done? Should not Tristan live in Marc's palace and be served by a hundred ladies? Should he not ride to the hunt and seek adventure and conquest? For me he is exiled from court, pursued in these woods, leading this life of a savage.'

"She heard Tristan's steps upon the leaves and went to meet him, removing, as was her custom, his sword.

" 'Dear one,' said Tristan, 'this is the sword of King Marc. It could have cut our throats. It spared us.'

"Iseut kissed the golden hilt and saw that Tristan wept.

" 'Tristan, my love,' she begged, 'let us make amends to Marc. But let us first return to the hermit Ogrin and pray the powerful King of Heaven for His mercy.'

"They awoke Gorvenal and all night they traveled for the last time through the beloved woods, no one speaking a word.

"When they reached the hermit's hut, Tristan took a vow. He vowed that he would go to a far land, and if some day the King wished him to return, he would serve him once again. Iseut knelt. 'I do not repent of having loved Tristan and loving Tristan, now and always,' she said, 'but our flesh, at least, from now on will be separated.'

"The hermit praised God for their salvation. Tristan left Iseut with him and set off for Tintagel with a message offering to return Iseut to the King. In the night he vaulted the orchard fence, as he had done in happier days, and stole to the King's window, calling softly.

"The King heard. 'Who are you that calls me in the night at such an hour?'

" 'Sire, I am Tristan. I bring you a message which I

am leaving here on the grill of this window. Farewell.'

" 'Tristan, Tristan, Tristan,' the King cried after him. But Tristan had fled. He regained the hermitage, where he found the hermit praying and Iseut weeping.

"After counseling with his barons and his chaplain, Marc sent word accepting Tristan's offer and sending also his love. On a day appointed, Tristan and Iseut came to the edge of the forest. In the distance they saw Marc and all his barons. 'My love,' said Tristan, 'what bitter grief to lose you.' He begged that if ever he sent her a message, she would do what the message asked.

" 'Dear friend,' Iseut replied, 'wear this jasper ring of mine for the love of me, and if ever a man comes to me with this ring, I shall know he comes from you and do your bidding—be it madness or wisdom. But in return, leave me your dog, Husdent; when I look at him, I will remember you and be less sad. And now hear my last prayer. You will go soon to a far land, but wait in the forest for a little while until I know for certain whether the King will treat me kindly. I will send word to you if anyone abuses me.'

"And he promised and took the ring, and she the dog, and they kissed each other on the lips.

"Then the King and all his retinue approached, their horses prancing and their pennants fluttering from their spears. Tristan gave Iseut to King Marc and turned and walked toward the sea. Marc would have given him a horse and gold and clothing, but Tristan would take nothing. Iseut watched until he was out of sight, but he did not look back.

"In a few days Andret and the other evil three came to Marc with new treachery. 'Your Majesty,' said Andret, 'recall that you once condemned the Queen without a trial. This was unjust. Now you have opportunity to let her justify herself. Since she is innocent, how could it harm her to swear on the bones of saints that she never dishonored you? And then to seize the hot iron, which all men know will not burn the hand of one who swears the truth. For so the custom is, and by this easy proof can Queen Iseut dispel all old suspicions.'

"Marc was angered and that night Iseut read his anger in his face. Suspecting danger, she drew from him the reason. 'Sire,' she said, 'on the tenth day from now I will prove my innocence by this trial your lords desire.'

"Then, secretly, Iseut sent a servant to Tristan with the news, asking that he attend the trial, disguised as a pilgrim.

"Now the plain where the trial was to be held in sight of all the people lay by a river. On the day appointed, the boat bearing Marc and Iseut sailed to the river bank, marshy and oozing with mud. Iseut said: 'How can I step ashore without soiling my long gown in the mire? Fetch me a carrier.' And one of the knights on shore hailed a poor pilgrim squatting on the bank and asked him to carry the Queen. The pilgrim took her in his arms and waded through the mire. 'Dear one,' she whispered low.

"A rich silken cloth was spread upon the grass and on it rested the relics of saints taken from caskets and shrines. Near them stood a burning pot of coals, wherein a whitely heated iron lay. The Queen, having prayed, removed the jewels from her neck and hands and gave them to beggars standing 'round. She took off her purple cape and headdress and her belt and shoes embroidered with precious gems. These also she gave to the poor. Wearing only her sleeveless white tunic, bare-armed and barefooted, she advanced toward the assembled nobles: 'You who are my witnesses, I swear, by these relics and by all the saints alive and dead, that never has man born of woman held me in his arms, except for my lord King Marc and that poor pilgrim there, who just now carried me to shore. King Marc, will that oath serve?'

" 'Yes, my Queen, and may God show the truth.'

" 'Amen,' said Iseut.

"Pale and unsteady, she approached the pot of coals. The crowd was still. Then she plunged her bare arms in the fire, seized the iron bar, walked nine steps holding it, threw it back into the fire, and held out her arms in the form of a cross, the palms of her hands upturned. And everyone could see that her flesh was smooth and whole as the finest fruit upon a tree. Then from all breasts a great cry of praise mounted to God.

"Yet again the lovers met. A few nights later, as Iseut lay sleepless in the arms of the sleeping Marc, she heard the plaintive voice of a nightingale, weaving a spell of song. And she remembered how thus, in the forest, Tristan had sung the songs of birds. This was he, then; this was his last farewell. How mournfully he called. 'My love,' she thought, 'never again shall I hear your voice.'

"The melody trembled still more ardently.

" 'Ah, what do you want? Do you want that I should come to you, Tristan? No, I cannot. Remember the hermit and the oaths we have sworn. Be quiet; death watches for us. But what matters death? You call me, you want me, I come.'

"She freed herself from the King's arms and threw a fur cape around her half-clothed body. In the corridor were ten guards, but all had fallen asleep on the floor. She stepped quietly over their forms and lifted the barrier on the door. The metal rasped but the guards slept fast. She stepped across the threshold into the night and the nightingale was quiet.

"Under the trees, without a word, Tristan pressed Iseut to his breast. Their arms locked around each other and until dawn they did not loosen the noose of love that held them as one.

"In the early morning, Tristan said: 'My love, I leave for I know not where. May the God born in Bethlehem guard you well.'

"'May He guard you too,' Iseut replied. 'My body stays here; my heart goes with you.'

"For two years Tristan and Gorvenal wandered through many lands, until they entered the land of Brittany. There they saw everywhere about them deserted villages, ruined walls, fields blackened and stubbled by fire. Their horses stirred clouds of cinders underfoot. For two days they rode without meeting a soul—not even a dog or a chicken. At noon on the third day they met a hermit dressed in goatskins. The hermit told them this was once a fair land, with many a farm, with windmills and orchards. The people were ruled by the good Duke Hoël. But a rebellious vassal of the Duke, one Riol, had conquered Brittany, carried off its riches as his prize, and burned the land. The Duke had been forced back to his castle, which any day now might be besieged.

"Tristan rode to the castle and offered the Duke his services, and was received to share the hardships of its lord. He met Kaherdin, the Duke's son, also the Duke's daughter, who was named Iseut of the White Hands. And Tristan smiled to hear that name again.

"In a very few days, just before dawn, the guards came running from the towers crying: 'Awake! Awake! Arm yourselves. Riol is here. The assault begins.'

"Knights rushed to the ramparts, and others followed Tristan and Kaherdin to battle at the gates. Tristan singled out Riol for attack, and so fierce was the duel that both horses were slain beneath their riders and the fighting finished on foot. Slashed to the skull by Tristan's sword, Riol begged mercy and surrendered. His men rode up to rescue him, but too late. Riol had given in. And Tristan made him swear fealty again to Hoël and go out and restore all the damage he had done in the land.

"After the battle Hoël took counsel with his nobles. Then, with their consent, he came to Tristan and said: 'Friend, I cannot thank you sufficiently, for you have saved Brittany. My daughter, Iseut of the White Lands, is born of dukes, descended from kings and queens. Take her. I give her to you in token of my gratitude.'

" 'My lord,' said Tristan, 'I will take her.' And the wedding was planned with royal pomp. But when the wedding night came, as servants disrobed Tristan, it happened that while tugging at his tight-sleeved tunic, they pulled from his finger the jasper ring which Iseut the Golden-Haired had given him. It fell clattering on the flagstone floor. And Tristan's mind was washed with wave upon wave of memories.

"He lay down beside the other Iseut, but he did not touch her. She heard him sigh. A little ashamed, she said: 'Dear Lord, have I offended you in some way? Why do you not give me even a single kiss? Tell me, that I may know my fault and try to make amends if so I can.'

" 'Friend,' replied Tristan, 'do not vex yourself. In other days, in another country, I almost died in battle with a dragon. I prayed for rescue to the Virgin Mother of God. I promised that if my life were saved that day, then when I married, I would for a year refrain from all embraces.'

" 'So then,' said Iseut of the White Hands, 'I will endure your vow with you—and gladly.' But in the morning, when the servants set upon her hair the head-dress of a married woman, she smiled sadly, thinking how little right she had to that attire.

"My noble lords and ladies, he who lives in sadness is like a man already dead. It was not only Iseut of the White Hands who was sad. Tristan languished in Brittany; he desired death but he wanted Iseut the Golden-Haired to know that if he died, he died for love of her. So once more to Cornwall.

"He left the castle secretly and on foot. Finding a vessel headed for Tintagel, he persuaded the sailors to take him aboard. On landing, he exchanged clothes with a fisherman, who was glad to give up his rough wear for the garments of a lord. Then Tristan cut his long hair off and shaved his head close, leaving a bald cross on top. He rubbed his face with magic herbs he had brought with him. So disguised was his complexion that no man could recognize him. He made a club of chestnut and hung it 'round his neck. Then, barefooted, he headed for the castle.

"The gate guard thought him a crazy fool and let him pass. Soldiers and servants crowded about him, ridiculing him and casting stones. With a laughing retinue, he reached the threshold of the hall where Marc and Iseut sat on a dais, playing chess.

"Amused, the King bade him enter. Tristan put on a show of antics. Then, voice disguised, he lightly proposed that the King give him the Queen, and in exchange, he would give his sister to the King.

"Marc laughed and said 'And where would you take the Queen?'

" 'Above, between the clouds and sky, to my lofty castle of glass. The sun lights it; the winds cannot shake it. I will keep the Queen there in a crystal room blossoming with roses, all glistening in the morning sun.'

" 'This is a clever fool,' murmured the barons. 'He is facile with words.'

" 'My friend,' said the King, playing with the jest, 'what makes you think my wife would pay attention to a hideous fool like you?'

" 'Your Majesty, I have the right to her. I have been through much for her and it is because of her that I became a fool.'

" 'Who are you then?'

" 'I am Tristan, who loves the Queen forever.'

"At that name Iseut paled and said: 'Who let you in here, evil fool? Your jokes do not please me, nor you either. No doubt you were drunk last night and your drunkenness has made you dream.'

" 'Yes,' replied the fool, 'I am drunk of a liquor that will never leave me. Iseut, do you not remember that warm day on the high seas? We were thirsty and we drank together from the same cup. Ever since, I have been drunk.'

"Iseut hid her face and stood up to leave. But the King caught hold of her ermine cape and made her sit down again. 'The fool is entertaining. Let us hear him to the end.'

"And Tristan told the whole story of his and Iseut's love. Afterward, shaken by memories, Iseut sobbed out to Brangien, 'That fool is a sorcerer. How else could he know what he knows?'

" 'Are you sure he is not Tristan himself?' asked Brangien.

" 'Go find him, Brangien. Look closely and see for yourself.' And Brangien went to seek the fool. He followed her and burst through Iseut's door. Still more memories he recounted: the meetings in the orchard, the life in the forest. And still Iseut did not know him.

"Finally he asked for his dog Husdent and when Brangien brought him, the dog bounded to his master, rolled at his feet, and licked his hands for joy. Then Tristan showed Iseut the jasper ring and Iseut knew her lover stood before her.

"But Tristan was grieved and angry. 'What does this ring matter?' he said in his own voice. 'Why did it take you so much longer than my dog to recognize me? How much more consoling would it have been to be known through the power of our love! Though my voice was disguised, you should have heard my heart.'

"And at the sound of his natural voice, the Queen fainted. When consciousness returned, she was in Tristan's arms, and he, repenting his sharpness, was kissing her eyes.

"The King and all the barons were much diverted by the fool who had wandered to their court. They gave him a hut to live in, that he might entertain them on command. And though they mocked and teased him, Tristan endured their raillery, being able from time to time to be with the Queen.

"But Andret suspected a fraud. He posted spies at the Queen's threshold. When Tristan appeared there, the spies started to chase him off, but he brandished his chestnut club so wildly in the air, they were afraid of his madness and let him pass. Inside, he told Iseut suspicions were aroused and he must flee.

" 'Dear one,' she said, 'wrap your arms so tightly about me that in the embrace our hearts will break and our souls fly away. Take me—not to the castle you jested about in court, but to that fortunate country you used to tell me of—the country from which no one returns, where musicians sing songs without end.'

" 'Yes, I will take you there,' Tristan replied, 'and in a time not long from now. When it arrives, I will call you. Iseut, will you come then?'

" 'You know I will,' she answered.

"When he left the room, the spies threw themselves on him. But he laughed and slung his club around and said, 'Why hold me, my lords? I have nothing more to do here, for my lady has sent me far away to make ready the castle I have promised her!' They let him go. And the fool, without hurrying, went off dancing."

The narrator in the castle hall at Poitiers has been speaking for a long time without pause. He stops now while the harpist plays a few mournful measures. There are tears in the eyes of many a lady listening. It is clear that the tale is reaching the climax which the narrator foretold in the beginning. He goes on:

"Shortly after Tristan returned to Brittany, he went out to do battle with seven brothers who had been making trouble for Kaherdin. Tristan killed all seven, but not before one brother had wounded him with a poisoned lance. The poison trickled through Tristan's veins and no doctor in all Brittany could cure him. His skin wasted and shrank taut on his bones and turned ghastly white.

"He knew that he was dying and called Kaherdin and asked him one last favor: fetch Iseut the Golden-Haired. And out of his love and gratitude, Kaherdin agreed. Tristan gave him the jasper ring and told him to disguise himself as a merchant of silks. While displaying goods to the Queen, Kaherdin could show her the ring and arrange for her to board his ship—and then set sail. Tristan told Kaherdin, too, many things about his love for Iseut in Cornwall and of the potion in which they had drunk love and death. And Kaherdin's heart was heavy for his friend.

" 'Return in forty days if you can,' Tristan adjured, 'and if you bring Iseut, hoist a white sail, but if you come alone, a black one.'

"Kaherdin told his sister, Iseut of the White Hands, that he would leave to seek a new doctor for Tristan in Cornwall. Then, gathering a crew, he departed.

"That other Iseut knew her brother lied. Hidden behind a partition, she had heard all that Tristan and Kaherdin had said. Nursing Tristan, she spoke sweetly and gave no sign, but waited for revenge.

"It was long before Kaherdin returned. A storm at sea blew his vessel off course. Tristan grew so feeble he could no longer leave his bed to watch for the ship with the white sail or the black. Each day he sent Iseut of the White Hands to the castle parapet to scan the sea. And one day she saw her brother's ship glide, white-sailed, to port. She hurried back to Tristan. 'My lord, Kaherdin comes. May he have with him the doctor who can cure you!'

" 'My good friend,' said Tristan, trembling, 'what color is the sail?'

"Iseut of the White Hands took her vengeance. 'It is black.'

"Tristan turned his face to the wall. 'I cannot hold on to my life longer,' he sighed. Then, three times: 'Iseut, Iseut, my dear. Iseut.' He would have spoken the name a fourth time, but in trying he died. And Iseut of the White Hands knew it was not her name he called.

"Quickly the sad news spread through the village and when Iseut the Golden-Haired stepped ashore, she heard great mourning in the streets, and bells pealing from chapels and monasteries.

"She asked a countryman for whom they knelled. He told her: 'Madam, for Tristan the loyal, Tristan the kind, Tristan the noble and generous.'

"Iseut spoke no word. Swiftly she climbed to the castle and as she sped, the Bretons marveled to look at her. Never had they seen a woman of such beauty.

"She found the other Iseut kneeling, shaken with sobs, by Tristan's bed. She said: 'Lady, get up and give me your place. I have more right to weep for him than you, believe me. I loved him more.'

"She turned toward the East and prayed. Then she

uncovered the body a little, lay down close beside it, and kissed the face and lips. Her body against his, her mouth on his, she gave up her soul, of grief.

"When news of the lovers' death reached Tintagel, Brangien told King Marc of the potion they had quaffed and how its magic sealed their fate. In pity and regret, the King crossed the sea to bring their bodies home.

"He had two coffins built, one of chalcedony for Iseut, the other of beryl for Tristan. He buried them beneath a chapel altar, one on the right and one on the left. During that night, a thornbush with green and leafy branches and fragrant flowers sprang from Tristan's tomb. It arched across the altar and plunged into Iseut's tomb. Churchkeepers cut it back, but on the next night, as green and flowering, as lively as before, new branches plunged again. Three times the churchkeepers tried to destroy the leaping bush. In vain. 'It is a miracle,' they said and told King Marc. The King forbade that anyone should cut the plant thereafter.

"And some say too that from the grave of Iseut sprang a shrub of roses which would not be kept back from Tristan's tomb.

"My noble lords and ladies, another may tell this tale another way. But, however told, it is a tale for lovers. May those among you who love in sadness find comfort in my story and those who love in gladness give thanks

for their joy. Now I have finished all that is written of
Tristan. May Christ accept it."

The story done, the narrator bows low with a flourish
of his cape. The orchestra strikes up, and if the night is
warm, the lords and ladies move out to the terrace to
stretch their legs and take a breath of fresh air after the
long recital. In the square tower of the nearby church
of Saint Porchaire, the bell, which by day calls university students to class, tinkles out the hour. The Countess
Marie calls the narrator to her side and rewards him with
a bag of coins. His listeners chat about his recitation
and then the talk turns to court matters. Servants move
from group to group, offering goblets of wine. The narrator assuages his dry throat, then slips off to his quarters in the Maubergeon tower of the castle, built by
Queen Eleanor's grandfather for a lovely lady friend,
La Maubergeonne. Glancing upward in the round, cozy
chamber, the narrator spies some gargoyles, humorous
miniature statues, which seem to wink at him from their
niches at ceiling level. Holding his candle high, he discovers they represent various professions. He snubs the
professor and the lawyer, but winks back at the magician
and the writer. Perhaps together they will inspire him
with a twist for a new tale he is devising for Marie.

TWO

The Real Tristans and Their Times

Had Tristan lived only as an example of castle theater, his story might be no more than a museum piece having extraordinary power to wring human hearts. But because his story blossomed from seeds of truth as well, Tristan remains a compelling mystery to those explorers of history's secrets who want to know who he really was.

Their pursuit of him begins among the Picts. Toward the end of the eighth century, the men of this tribe in the northeast of what is now Scotland were fighting for

their lives, their wives, and their not inconsiderable store
of silver, gold, and gems.

Down the North Sea from Scandinavia came the
enemy in long, narrow, high-prowed boats, each with a
single square sail billowing from its single mast. The
gunwales were laden with the lindenwood shields of
Vikings—twenty mail-shirted warriors to a boat. A
dozen oarsmen, six to the starboard and six to the lee-
ward, tugged at their oars to assist the wind. Swiftly the
vessels skimmed to shore. Landing, the sailors became
soldiers. They stole the first horses they could find and
headed for churches and monasteries. In these sanctuar-
ies were the richest of Pictish riches: the silver and gold
caskets, jewel-studded, in which the monks kept their
handwritten books; the staff of the head monk, set with
gems; golden incense burners and hanging torches that
swung on silver chains.

When the plunderers had gathered this loot, they gal-
loped to the circular villages in which the Picts lived,
hoping to capture the beautiful Irish wives which many
of them possessed. They carried women and bounty
back to their boats, butchering men and cattle and
burning the land behind them—unless, of course, a Pictish watchman, from the top of a *broch*, a round stone-
tower, sighted the invaders at sea in time to rouse the
defense. Then the Picts would pack their wives and children into the broch and launch their animal-hide boats
to meet the invaders. Many a day in the prow of the

commanding boat must have stood King Drust of Pictavia, metal shield at his bare breast, the animal tattoos on his body quivering as he flexed his muscles. He was attired like his men, in nothing more than the bronze armlets which supported his biceps and helped him deliver death-dealing blows with his stone club.

King Drust was a fighting monarch who probably reigned from A.D. 780 to 785. In old Pictish chronicles and monkish histories, Drust's name was spelled in various ways, as was common in ancient records. One of the alternate spellings, Drystan, intrigues Tristan detectives, for a trace of such a name together with the name Drust has been found in territory known to have been ruled by Marc of Cornwall. Moreover, Tristan is thought by many language experts to be just another spelling of Drystan. This and other evidence leads to a generally accepted conclusion that the legendary Tristan was, in part, the Pictish monarch's namesake.

Of King Drust little is recorded beyond his ancestry and the high regard in which he was held, but enough is known of his people and his times to let us imagine in what ways he earned his subjects' devotion. He had not only to ward off Norse invaders but to repel attacks from an English kingdom to the south, Northumbria, and from the Scoti, or Scotch, to the west. Even among Pictish clans, quarrels over land and religion burst into clashes. The Picts had been converted from nature-worship to Christianity some two centuries earlier by a

British saint, Ninian, and an Irish saint, Columba. Ninian and Columba disagreed on articles of faith, and their followers kept the argument burning.

Drust was probably quick to rescue other monarchs in trouble, partly because royal standards required him to, and partly perhaps because he lived never knowing when he himself might need such succor in return. An ancient Irish account tells of a Pictish Drust who with another hero freed a kingdom in the Hebrides Islands, off Pictavia's coast, from the necessity of delivering its youth to foreign bondage—the same threat from which Tristan freed Marc.

Between battles, the Picts were gentlefolk who lived elegantly, for their times. King Drust's Queen wove material for his garments from the spun wool of the clan's sheep or from vegetable fibers dyed in glowing colors. Only in combat did the Picts prefer to be unencumbered by clothing. In peacetime they wore inner and outer garments, the latter with long, flowing sleeves and hoods. The King alone wore tight sleeves and straight lines to the ankles, the garb of royal blood. His Queen fashioned them with her bone needle. Like other men, he no doubt fancied bronze pendants, and she, like other women, favored bone ornaments in her high-coiled hair, which she held in position with bone hairpins.

Drust would have been a very democratic king. He had to be, for he had been elected by his clan after the death of his father. It was the custom of the clan to decide by vote which of the King's sons should rule. Should a king be childless, the clan might choose one of his sister's sons, or the son of a daughter of a previous king. The royal Pict line descended through women, in accordance with a promise made to the Irish by the first Picts who took Irish wives.

Drust lived in the chief village of his own clan, his house set a little apart from the others, fenced with pointed stakes like the orchard behind Tintagel. His village may have been in Loone, now the Scottish province of Lothian (in the legend, Lyonesse). An early English historian tells how Loone was besieged by a rebellious lord, one Morgan, of the same name as the enemy baron who slew Tristan's father and stole his inheritance.

Other clans in other regions of Pictavia were governed by *thanes*, who were responsible to Drust and who turned in to his *althane*, or royal treasurer, the taxes they collected. From time to time, Drust summoned his thanes, to listen to their reports of the state of the nation. After the council, thanes and monarch might ride to the chase in quest of deer. It is likely Drust was as good a shot as Tristan, for noble youths were taught from childhood to make and handle well their willow bows and arrows. Tracking otters was another royal sport. Its object was to find the fish the otters hunted. In the otters' hunting grounds, Drust doubtless set his willow traps or speared salmon with his stone-tipped lance.

He and his people ate well, from shapely pottery. They grew their own grain and ground their own flour. Their mills turned only toward the sun; none could be budged in the opposite direction. The moving parts of all Pictish tools revolved sunwise. This peculiarity is one way scientists who excavate old ruins tell whether implements they find in Scottish soil today once belonged to Picts. No one knows why Picts wanted their tools to move toward light, or why their conical, animal-skin-roofed houses always faced south. This is the way it was in Pictavia.

Drust's house was stone, like those of his thanes and other nobles. Many of his subjects built their houses with tree trunks hewn from the forest. In every village, in the morning, children were hurried out the doors facing south, their mothers urging them on lest they be late for school. Schooling was important to the Picts. Monks taught the children to read and write and figure and behave. The Pictish code of behavior was simple but strict. The rules were: Always give food and shelter to a stranger, protect women and the weak, be loyal to one's ruler and reverent toward *Dis*, God; be courteous to all; be brave. Essentially, this idea of goodness was the same that prevailed in the Middle Ages and in the circles where Tristan moved. As winner of the Picts' esteem, Drust must have exemplified this code like the true king he was.

Often at night he and his Queen would have been

entertained with heroic tales of tribal triumphs told by bards. Afterwards, the bard might be rewarded with a rich trinket from a Roman trading ship, purchased with coins which Drust's metal workers had made.

This civilization over which Drust reigned—fierce in battle, gentle in peace—lost its identity in the ninth century when the Scoti conquered and absorbed the Picts. By then King Drust had long been buried under a high-heaped mound of stones or one of the pointed rocks which signified that the dust below was noble. Little was left to remember him by, but through the Tristan legend his name was destined to be mingled with the names of other nobles, noted by chroniclers of other ages, in other kingdoms.

Who were these nobles? That question has raised a host of others and started lively arguments among experts.

Archaeologists who dig in old ruins, philologists who decipher old languages, interpreters of folklore, geologists, geographers, and historians have pursued the identity of Tristan like a pack of sleuths, each from a different angle. To follow their tracks, it's necessary to know the England and France of the time when the legend was being formed and some of the scholars of that day whose records today's scholars have searched. The hundred years between the middle of the eleventh and of the twelfth century have yielded the Tristan detectives their richest clues.

The central figure of that age was William the Conqueror. French-born, he earned his title by invading England in 1066, defeating the heir to the English throne, and seizing it for himself.

This famous figure of history came naturally by his zest for conquest. He grew up in an age of skulduggery and sword-brandishing, when kings were weak and dukes were strong and rival dukedoms schemed to devour their neighbors. His father, Robert, Duke of Normandy, was the strongman of northern France. Neighboring Brittany, between feuds among its own dukes, tried to take over Robert's lands. Instead, Duke Robert conquered Brittany. Then he made the mistake of leaving the scene to embark on one of the Crusades in which European Christians hoped to capture Jerusalem from the Moslems, incidentally looting the riches of the East. William, then a baby of three months, was left in the care of a Breton lord, Alain. Robert died during the Crusade; Alain was mysteriously poisoned. Alain's wife, the Lady Berthe, tried to protect the infant, but an uncle, eager for William's inheritance, kidnapped him. By the time he was fifteen, William, aware of his rights and how to maintain them, assembled an army and declared himself Duke of Brittany and Normandy. He fought the army of his uncle for six years, until at the age of twenty-one he made his title secure. At thirty-nine he took the throne of England and changed the course of English history.

The kings who followed William claimed large parts of France, and French became the language of educated Englishmen. The cultures and customs of the two countries were interwoven. These changes didn't strike William's subjects as abrupt, however. Even before the conquest, comings and going between the dukedoms of northern France and southern England had been so frequent as to make people on either side of the English Channel feel at home with one another. Both regions had been settled by Celts who has crossed Europe centuries before Christ. Even after the Celts became Christians, their lively tribal folklore flourished, and even after they had been conquered by other tribes, the folklore remained embedded in Breton-Norman-British tradition. Moreover, Bretons and Normans had British relatives. The English king whose throne William mounted was the grandson of a Norman woman.

Geoffrey of Monmouth, one of the principal historians who influenced the formation of the Tristan legend in the early twelfth century, was of Breton descent and confesses in the preface to his *History of the Kings of Britain* that he took some of his material "from a very old book in the Breton tongue." Geoffrey worked as a clerk at Oxford University during the reign of William the Conqueror's grandson, Henry II. He wrote his *History* at the King's command. It was more romantic than accurate, because, as was common practice among recorders of the day, he frequently rearranged, exaggerated, sometimes even fabricated incidents and dates in the hope of flattering and entertaining His Majesty.

A record which has yielded more reliable Tristan clues is the Domesday Book. This is a ledger of English land ownership which William the Conqueror, soon after his arrival in England, caused to be composed for tax purposes. William was interested in money, not romance. The Domesday Book was required to be accurate—or woe to the clerks assigned to the task. The account lists the castle of Marc, who in real life was a duke of Cornwall in southwest England. His castle was not the gleaming Tintagel of the legend. Rather, it was a fort-like structure of earthwork called Castle Dor. It stood near the Fowey River, about forty miles from the bluff where the ruins of Tintagel today tumble toward the sea.

Not until 1145, more than four centuries after the latest date assigned by modern historians to Marc and his times, did Tintagel become a castle. Its oldest quarters were built by Celtic monks to serve as their retreat, perhaps as long ago as A.D. 500. The monks worked with the flat pieces of shingle-like slate that still slide down the Cornish hillsides. Having no cement, they piled the loose slate, piece on piece, into precarious walls. Miraculously some of their walls survive, along with the weighty rectangular stone block which was their chapel altar.

In 1145 one Reginald, Earl of Cornwall, raised his castle where the monastery had been, incorporating such of its ruins as remained. The monks had long since dispersed. Reginald's castle also crumbled and later other nobles built homes, each on the ruins of the others. Today the whole assembly stands upon a headland which the fuming sea has very nearly split in two. Down one cliff, then up the next, fragments of Tintagel's past are scattered through patches of grass, spongy English moss, and prickly yellow gorse. Often the fragments are indistinguishable from natural boulders and pinnacles of the cliffs. No matter if Tristan never wooed Iseut here; there is a stretch behind the fallen walls, once a monastic or ducal garden, that could have been the likeness of the orchard where the pair sought the shelter of the night. There is even a bubbling spring that through the severest droughts has never dried!

The bestowal of Tintagel on Marc by authors of the Tristan legend was due to the influence and popularity of Geoffrey of Monmouth's fanciful history. Geoffrey's sponsor, King Henry, was the half brother of Tintagel's rebuilder, the Duke of Cornwall. Thus, Geoffrey had come to know Tintagel. Seeking to flatter the royal family, Geoffrey decided to give the castle a noble origin. He made it the abode of King Arthur and his

Table Round of Knights. Arthur, a legendary monarch surrounded by knights whose mission was to fight evil, was in actual life a Celtic general surrounded by soldiers whose mission was to fight Anglo-Saxon tribes. Malory exaggerated him into a hero of English history, crowned him for all time, and installed him within Tintagel's ramparts. Tristan bards, seeking a popular setting for their romance, appropriated Arthur's headquarters for Marc.

Tintagel lends itself to legend. Seeming to possess the enchanted spell Iseut whispered of to her lover in the orchard, it becomes what men wish to believe—a stronghold in their hearts, impregnable.

By contrast, the wind-battered, bracken-and-bramble-tufted mounds which are all that remain of Castle Dor retain the more rugged atmosphere that, in reality, the lovers must have known. In the shape of horseshoes, double embankments slant upward from a wheat field. The inner embankment was once an Iron Age stockade. Much later, between 50 B.C. and A.D. 80, it was incorporated in a Celtic fort. The outer mound is what remains of an addition made sometime between A.D. 500 and 900, when Marc is believed to have made this his castle. His great hall, ninety feet long and forty feet wide, occupied the central space. Here he held his councils with his barons, and his feasts. Here Tristan would have delivered Marc's bride.

Tristan's ship would have sailed up the Fowey River,

landing not far from the foot of the castle. Here too he would have landed when first he came to Cornwall and again when he returned from Brittany, for in his time the upper Fowey, now only a tiny tidal stream, was a powerful waterway, heavy with sea traffic from near and far.

The castle was strategically placed to guard this entranceway. It also commanded wide inland views over the moors to the mountains. A modern road leading inland passes the castle and follows the same artery used by early Britons, Celts, Breton traders, and Normans traveling north from Fowey harbor and then westward to the Atlantic coast. Little could move in this corner of England, by land or sea, unobserved from Marc's stronghold.

Even now it's a formidable scramble to clamber up into the old earthworks. Once on top, you see and hear sights and sounds that could have been familiar to Tristan's eyes and ears. Southeast is the blue triangle where the Fowey meets the sea. The fields of half of Cornwall circle the castle and climb away into the distant hills. They are farmed now, as once they were for castle occupants. Depending on the season, the farm meadows may be patched with golden gorse and the hedgerows between them white with blackberry blooms or blushing with primroses. Now, as then, wind sighs in the wheat and gulls call from the sea.

A modern note is the slither of tires on the asphalt

road beyond the hedgerow that hides the ruins. Passing autos soon come to a crossroads where they veer around a curious granite stone. Set in a central oasis of grass and wildflowers, it points skyward like a stalagmite. Dug into one side of it is an early T-shaped form of the Christian cross. Faintly inscribed in Latin on the other side is "Drystan lies here, son of Cunomorus." (According to ninth-century church records, Cunomorus was an alternate Welsh name for Marc. The records refer to him as "Marc, called Cunomorus.")

A second stone in the neighborhood, about a mile and a half from the castle, commemorates "Drust, son of Cunomorus." Do these carvings mean that Tristan was in reality Marc's son and not, as in the legend, his nephew? Are Drystan and Drust one and the same, the Drust of Pictavia? Many language sleuths think so. And the folklore detectives believe it quite likely that the first bards to build Tristan's tale, considering it unseemly for their hero to steal his father's bride, made him Marc's nephew instead.

But historians who have pieced together Domesday listings and other ancient records disagree. They deduce that King Drust of Pictavia was indeed the son of Marc's sister and that Marc himself was of Pictish-Celtic ancestry. There being no record of Marc having children, they suggest that Drust, according to Pictish rules of inheriting through women, was elected his heir. They submit that the early bards were familiar with these facts and interpreted them dramatically by having Marc desire to make Tristan his heir, thus running into conflict with his jealous barons.

These same historians refuse to attach any special importance to the stones near Castle Dor. According to them, the names Drust or Drystan and Cunomorus were too common in the sixth century—which is when archaeologists say the stones were carved—to prove with certainty for whom the monuments were engraved. Furthermore, they claim that Marc lived in the eighth century, not the sixth. They identify him as a duke, renowned for doughty defense against the Norse raids on Cornwall, which were most severe in the eighth and ninth centuries. Iseut, they believe, may well have been Îswalt, a golden-haired Viking princess of Ireland, which the Vikings at that time held in thrall. These historians have deciphered evidence that the hand of such a princess in marriage was a prize which Marc's prowess permitted him to win from the raiders he repelled.

Other historians are dubious. Why then, they ask, do old Breton histories make Marc of Cornwall a sixth-century hero? The eighth-century defenders are ready with their reply: the reason is that Bretons vaunted the sixth century as the Golden Age when Celts settled Brittany. Breton fanciers of the Malory type moved Marc back two hundred years to conform to their calendar of glory.

Folklore scholars suggest another possibility. An ancient Welsh saga, the *Mabinogien,* refers to a General Drystan, commander of the army of a Welsh king of a still earlier time—the fifth century. The King's name is much like Marc's: he was called King March. The old saga narrates that the King had the pointed ears of the devil. Folklorists say that Marc's other Welsh name, Cunomorus, really meant Prince of Darkness, a title often given to the devil. In Celtic, Marc meant horse, and in some early versions of the Tristan romance Marc is given horse's ears. The Celts, say these folklorists, may have taken the basic pattern of ears-to-match-a-name from the Welsh and remodeled it in a fashion familiar to their listeners. In the *Mabinogien,* the King and his general are far from heroic figures. They spend more time guarding pigs than governing or defending a kingdom. Thought most of the saga is considered pure fancy, it is nevertheless important as the source from which Geoffrey of Monmouth dug out the Arthur myth. It is important to the Tristan legend because some of its elements also found their way into that account, adding a new layer of disguise to the identity of the hero. And across the Irish Sea from Wales, the first Tristan storytellers found more grist for their mill. They borrowed from Irish tales to enhance the magic powers of their hero and to weave the fateful quality of his romance.

Small wonder that with so much borrowing and

reweaving in the dim haze of ages past, the location of even Tristan's birthplace, Lyonesse, is today a subject of debate. Many historians who have joined the search for it propose Lothian, in Scotland, as the likely site, but as many geographers doubt that. More likely, they suggest he was born in a kingdom that now lies fifty fathoms under the sea, beyond Land's End, where the southwest tip of Cornwall—and all England—pierces the Atlantic. There great boulders have somersaulted toward the surf. Some, having been halted, rest there, still teetering on the steep shore. Others have rolled miles out to form an underwater plateau. The geographers call geologists to their rescue. Yes, say the geologists, this plateau may once have risen above the waves that now rise above it. Lyonesse, Lyonesse!

Between Land's End and the Fowey River lies the setting for Tristan's love affair with Iseut the Golden-Haired. On this one point, scholars have no arguments. Domesday Book descriptions of the Forest of Morois and others of the lovers' haunts parallel precisely the locale of the legend.

There is also little doubt surrounding the Breton setting of Tristan's life with the other Iseut. Here enters another historical personage from whom the legend of Tristan borrows: one Triscan, a renowned Lord of

Vitré, a Breton contemporary of William the Conqueror. Lord Triscan's lands lay hard on the border of Brittany and Normandy, and they were a frequent battlefield for the forces struggling for power during William's youth.

When Tristan and Gorvenal crossed Brittany and came to the rescue of the good Duke Hoël, living with his family in fear behind his castle walls, Tristan's heart was struck by "deserted villages, fields blackened and stubbled." An actual report of the time reads: "News of the approach of a count, a duke, a king, causes the people to quake. By any high-born presence, they know they are menaced. The villagers bury whatever is precious. If God has blessed their wives and daughters with beauty, they send them away. The cities will not admit a retinue within their walls until agreement has been reached on a rapid departure. Workers set about tearing up roads in advance of a royal arrival. Farmers flood their fields, turning them to bogs to prevent passage, or burn them to deny food to the retinue. By every means possible, one isolates oneself."

Geographically as well as in history, Brittany made an ideal setting for the castle overlooking the sea where Iseut of the White Hands watched from the parapets for the ship with the black sail or the white. Brittany's is a jagged coastline, cleft by deep inlets, guarded by promontories against which the turquoise sea batters itself to snowy foam. The promontories rise in natural terraces of brown rock.

On the crest of one of these, near the village of Saint Lunaire, are the remains of rambling battlements of some old fort or abbey or castle. No one knows which. Parts are just piled stone, like Tintagel. Fishermen surfcast from the lower terraces, the collars of their yellow oilskin slickers turned up, the brims of their oilskin hats turned down against sheets of cascading spray. Back from the promontory grow fields of fern, shoulder-high, where wild roses and geraniums bloom in spring.

It is easy to imagine that other Iseut on such a point, watching for a ship, or even, like some French-tellers of the legend, to conclude that Tristan's Lyonesse was not Loone or a sunken land but Brittany—of course! In some rocky stronghold like Saint Lunaire one can conceive of the young Tristan, hidden from his father's enemy by Gorvenal, learning to ride and hunt through the fern, to leap from shelf to shelf along the terraced rock. Histories of Breton feuds, such as those that threatened the child William the Conqueror, could easily inspire a medieval French romancer with the idea for the threat to the boy Tristan and could further reinforce the notion of Brittany as Lyonesse.

That is just a notion, say the fact-searchers, while

freely admitting that Sir Tristan, having crossed the
Channel, adopted French background and French locale.
His legend traveled the length of the land, becoming
ever more popular as it passed from court to court.
Whoever the first Tristan was, or whatever combination
of men, wherever born and raised, all who wrote of him
found in the fragments which sparked their tales these
things in common: he was brave, no matter what the
risks; he was a faithful lover, no matter that the cost of
love was death.

Part II

HOW THE LEGEND GREW

Entre ceus ky solent cunter
E del cunte Tristan parler,
Ils en cuntent diversement:
Oï en ai de plusieur gent.
Asez sai que chescun en dit
E ço k'il unt mis en escrit....

Among bards skilled to weave romance
Who tales of Tristan to enhance,
None quite the same tale does unfold:
I have myself heard many told.
I know what each has had to say
And all their writings can convey.

From Roman de Tristan, *by*
Thomas, 1170

THREE

Sir Tristan
Travels

Who was first to write down Tristan's story? Searchers
for the truth have often been led astray by their own
patriotism. French scholars have hoped to prove that
Tristan leapt from tongue to pen in their country; Eng-
lish-speaking scholars hope that some part of Britain can
claim this honor.

There is no question but that French, English, Scotch,
Welsh, and Irish myths, as well as the actual deeds of
old-time heroes in the isles of Britain and in northern
France, are all recorded by the romance. Through study

these elements can be neatly pinned down. Not so the
name of that original scribe who, his head ringing with
long-ago lore, sharpened his goose quill, dipped it in
oak-sap ink, and scraped onto animal-hide parchment
the episodes that suited him best. The Anglo-Norman
poet Thomas wrote the earliest surviving narrative, but
he did not write the first one. He himself says, in a con-
tinuation of the passage on p. 68:

Mais selun ço j'ai oï
Nel dient pas selun Breri,
Ky solt les gestes e les cuntes
De tuz les reis, de tuz les cuntes
Ky orent este en Bretaigne.

But 'mongst all those whom I have heard
Breri spoke the truest word,
Who knew the tales of love and swords
Of all the kings and noble lords
Of days gone by in Britain.

The Breri to whom Thomas doffed his hat with a poetic
flourish is the same whom—along with Thomas and
Chrétien de Troyes—you met in the beginning of this
book at the court of Eleanor of Aquitaine. Although
some Tristan sleuths doubt if Breri wrote his version
down, many others credit him with being, if not the
first, at least among the very first to record Tristan's
adventures. Still others believe that the forerunner of

medieval authors like Thomas was a French romancer, name unknown, birthdate uncertain.

However sharp these differences, the scholarly sleuths do agree that Breri, Bleddri, Bleheri, or Blehericus—as that gentleman was variously known—had a lasting influence on his successors. Breri was a red-headed Welsh storyteller of the early twelfth century. He became a great friend of England's Norman rulers, who, although they robbed him of much of his land, gave him a title—Lord of Cilsant—and a royal job as the official conveyer of the King's commands to his Welsh country-men. He obviously made himself useful to those in high places, for he was also a good friend of the powerful Count of Poitou in France, the grandfather of Eleanor.

Both Breri and Thomas were familiar figures at Eleanor's own court in Poitiers, and Thomas was one of her special favorites. It is believed that he may well have written his Tristan for her, in 1170 or thereabouts. Of Thomas's life and circumstances we know almost noth-ing. His courtly style shows that he was fully at ease in noble society, and his command of language reveals that he had very likely been university-trained as a church scribe.

We know more about that other court bard, Chrétien de Troyes, who was the darling of Eleanor's daughter, Princess Marie. Chrétien wrote his Tristan some five years before Thomas was moved to adopt the theme, but we can only guess from Chrétien's other successes how he saw fit to present his Tristan. The manuscript has perished. Perhaps he himself destroyed it, for although the *story* of Tristan and Iseut fascinated him, he disapproved of Tristan and Iseut themselves. He wrote about them when he was very young. As he grew older, his work grew more prim and proper and the lovers' abandon to their love must have irked him, even while it haunted him. Tristan reappears in several tales; he would not let Chrétien go.

Besides reservations about the lovers' ardor, Chrétien must have been troubled by the magic potion which set their love aflame. He disliked having his characters molded by supernatural forces. Rather, he let their actions follow from the kind of people they were. Out of Chrétien's conflict between being attracted and repulsed by Tristan came his masterpiece, a novel called *Cliges*, in which he transposed the Tristan theme to another setting. *Cliges* was what Chrétien thought Tristan should be. In it the lovers, by other names, are free agents, and although they do very nearly what Tristan and Iseut did, they do it with greater restraint and end up a married couple, living happily ever after. *Cliges* won for the author, in later times, the title "inventor of the modern novel."

Like Thomas, Chrétien also mentions Breri. He probably first met Breri in England, where he had traveled in search of a sponsor and was adopted by Eleanor during

the years when she reigned there as Henry II's Queen.
The writer uses the royal couple's castle at Windsor as a
gala setting for one of his stories. While in England, he
may have collected the Pictish lore that enlivens his
storytelling. He may also have pored over Geoffrey of
Monmouth's tales of King Arthur, if he had not already
thrilled, as a boy, to one of their French translations. He
tried his own pen with Arthurian legend in several
books, recalling Tristan to life as a friend of Arthur's
knights.

From study of his travels and writing, scholars suspect that Chrétien's lost Tristan must have been an ele-
gant melding of Pictish and Celtic chronicles, flavored
with Arthurian dash and smoothed out with the sophisticated ideals of courtly love fashionable among the
noble audiences of his day.

Chrétien wrote always for noble sponsors: Eleanor,
her daughter, Princess Marie, and later for the ruler of
the state of Flanders. Often he must have suffered from
inevitable conflict between royal tastes and his own, for
his food, shelter, and stipend depended on writing to
suit his sponsors, yet he himself was a creative and dis-
criminating craftsman, with a sense of plot and drama
too advanced for his time. When the Princess Marie
hung over his shoulder, as she sometimes did, practically
dictating what lines he should set down, Chrétien must
have been very hungry in order to put up with her. Or
perhaps he shuddered even more at the thought of the

alternative: the church clerking for which he had been trained and which he had found so dull. He had come a long way from Troyes, the little town of many churches, to the southeast of Paris where he had been born. He never ceased to work at going still further. Ambitious, gifted, stick-to-itive, he labored hard and late and died with his pen in his hand.

To what extent Tristan chroniclers who followed Chrétien may have drawn on his genius, no one can tell. The Tristan of Thomas is polished smooth; that of Béroul, whose version appeared toward the end of the twelfth century, is rough and primitive, yet moving in its starkness. A mere fragment remains, and our knowledge of its author is even more fragmentary. We know only that he was one of those rebellious students, irked by classical studies in the university, where he, like so many others, was being prepared for a church career. He quit because he wanted to become a popular writer. Thereafter he made his living as a *jongleur*, a wandering minstrel.

Thomas, Chrétien, and Béroul wrote in French, for French-speaking audiences. At about the same time that Thomas's version was being related in the courts of France, a German, Eilhart von Oberg, presented *Tristrant* to his countrymen. Eilhart was a very different kind of man from the educated French narrators who had preceded him. Although he came from a family of minor nobles, he had had little if any schooling. His home was in the German state of Saxony, which at that time had not caught up with the learning and cultured tastes of nobility in the rest of Europe. Eilhart couldn't even read! But he could rhyme. The wife of the ruling Duke of Saxony was teen-aged Mathilde, a daughter of Eleanor. It was for her that Eilhart rhymed the Tristan romance, of which—perhaps homesick for the good times at her mother's court—she had undoubtedly given him the gist. Eilhart had accompanied her and her husband on a long visit to Normandy during a period when the duke, having supported the losing side in civil fights in Germany, thought it politic to travel for his health. It is entirely possible that Eilhart had picked up on this journey the Celtic folklore that is the heart of the plot.

Unlike Béroul, however, Eilhart feared the naked form of Celtic chronicles. He wanted his poem to please not only the young Mathilde but more staid ears as well. Consequently, he played down the fierceness of the lovers' devotion. The result must have grieved Mathilde. It is neither rough-hewn Celtic gem nor, like Thomas's courtly tale, buffed to a dazzle. It's dull wood. For example, when Iseut falls in love with Tristan, she exclaims: "It is a hard fate that has befallen me!" The love scenes are passed over quickly. Eilhart's favorite way of describing them, whether on the boat approaching Cornwall, in the Tintagel orchard, or in the forest of Morois, is to state that the lovers had "much joy." Occasionally, he goes so far as to permit "great joy," but never does he convey the flaming feeling of the French versions, in which the lovers "gave themselves up wholly to their love," and love "pressed them harder every day, as thirst presses a stag to the stream or hunger plummets a hawk to its prey."

After Eilhart, as the twelfth century gave way to the thirteenth, version upon version of the lovers' tragedy swept from court to court, country to country. Tristan and Iseut became the Romeo and Juliet of the day. Most of the rehashes lacked distinction, but one, borrowed from Thomas in 1220 by Gottfried von Strassburg, was to be lifted to distinction by a gifted German composer more than six hundred years later. Richard Wagner based his opera, *Tristan und Isolde,* on Gottfried's poem, rewriting it to suit his ideas and his music. The result is still a favorite in the world's great opera houses.

In 1230 came an interpretation charming in its own right: the melodic *Honeysuckle Song,* from the pen of Eleanor's sister-in-law, Marie de France. Along with the many versions came translations. Eilhart's verses were translated into Czechoslovakian, Thomas's into English. Jongleurs put other versions into Spanish and Italian. The King of Norway, Haakon V, commissioned a monk, Brother Robert, to introduce the lovers to his court. In 1226 Brother Robert paraphrased Thomas in Norwegian. And so it came about, mainly through the inspiration passed on by that obscure but urbane scribe, Thomas, and owing much to the encouragement of a connoisseur Queen, Eleanor of France and England, and her family, that Sir Tristan traveled over land, sea, and time.

He traveled not only in the written and spoken word but in the art of the tilemaker and the painter and the ivory carver, the skill of the tapestry weaver. Noble families demanded tiles, tapestries, table covers, ivory coffers, murals, silken hangings, and bedspreads illustrating scenes from Tristan and Iseut. Some of these have been rediscovered, the color and carving freshly evoking the scenes from the story which were most beloved by its early fans: the lovers' trysts, the trial of Iseut, the conquests of Tristan, the double death and the flowering graves.

The most famous set of illustrations is the collection of tiles in the British Museum, catalogued as "one of the finest, if not *the* finest, inlaid pavement in existence." The tiles were discovered in 1853 in the ruins of an abbey near Chertsey, England, by Dr. Manwaring Shurlock, a surgeon whose hobby was poking around ruins for finds from ages past. Dr. Shurlock's discovery brought professional excavators rushing to the scene. They found many of the tiles paving the floor of what was once the abbey pigsty; others lay broken in the soil. Some had been carted off centuries earlier and are now in old estate houses and church chancels.

The tiles are round, with borders of flowers, curlicues, dragons, and signs of the zodiac. The outermost border of each is an inscription which captions the scene inside. The scenes were taken from Thomas. Language experts aren't sure whether the inscriptions are old French or the very similar Anglo-Norman speech derived from it in Old England.

The material is the red clay of the neighboring hills. Monks molded this, stamped it with patterns, and filled the depressions in the patterns with a white clay. Then they glazed the whole with transparent yellow lead and loaded pansful into their potter's oven. In the baking process, chemicals in the clay turned the surface dark green, red-brown, black. The colors still keep their somber glow.

Doubtless the paving wasn't meant for the pigsty or anywhere else in the abbey. More likely the monks' work had been commissioned for a palace. Scholars hazard the guess that it was the palace of King Henry III of England, Eleanor's grandson, a lover of fine arts to whom the Tristan story would very likely be known. What interrupted delivery of the King's order, nobody knows.

Other magnificent Tristan décor exists in other countries. In Germany, Eilhart's Tristan was the theme for a twenty-two-scene tapestry, now in a convent near Hannover, and a twenty-six-scene tablecloth, prized by the town of Erfurt. In the castle of Saint Floret, near the village of Issoire in southern France, are forty murals believed to illustrate Chrétien's lost manuscript.

In the Austrian Tyrol, more murals adorn the walls of Castle Runkelstein with paintings of Gottfried von Strassburg's story. In a Russian museum in Petrograd an ivory coffer with forty scenes from Thomas is displayed. The coffer is an import from northern France. And these are only a few of the museum treasures that keep before modern eyes—as they did before those of thirteenth- and fourteenth-century castle dwellers—the tale inherited from generations past.

In 1485 an English writer, Sir Thomas Malory, set down the version which was to guarantee Tristan his future in English literature. Sir Thomas, for a while a member of the British Parliament, lived during bad times for his country. The War of the Roses was tearing England apart. With a white rose as their insignia, the dukes of the House of York fought the warriors of the red rose, the dukes of the House of Lancaster. The prize both houses sought was the throne of all England. While the contest raged through the countryside, government went to the winds. The people fended for themselves as best they could and tried to evade jail when their means were illegal.

Sir Thomas was no exception. He stole cattle, deer, and horses, and robbed an abbey. Less successful than some others in escaping the consequences, he was known in almost every London prison. Sometimes he served out his sentences. Twice he escaped: once by leaping into the moat, a deep ditch of water that surrounded the jail,

and swimming to freedom; another time by overcoming
the guards. He shifted sides between the roses, fighting
now for the white, now for the red, depending on
which one he thought was gaining the upper hand. His
writing, all done in prison, is a supreme contrast to his
life. He turned out a twenty-one-volume history, *The
Birth, Life and Acts of King Arthur and of the Noble
Knights of the Round Table*, better known as the *Morte
d'Arthur*. Based mainly on Geoffrey of Monmouth, it
was intended as a reminder to readers of the greatness of
their country in former days and, at the end, when
Arthur dies, as a moral warning against breakdowns in
law and order. The King and his knights set examples of
honor and piety, wisdom and justice.

In addition to Monmouth's Arthurian lore, Malory
had read a French prose Tristan which had appeared in
1230. Like some earlier Tristan narratives, this one had
made Tristan a contemporary of King Arthur. Malory
went further. He dubbed Tristan a Knight of the
Round Table. Three of his twenty-one volumes of
Round Table deeds are devoted to Sir Tristram and
la beale Isoud, his names for the lovers. At the end of
the third volume, the couple are living, sufficient unto
themselves, in Joyous-Gard, a castle loaned them by the
bravest of Arthur's knights, Sir Lancelot. Thither
Tristram has transported *la beale*, after having stolen

her from Tintagel. In order to justify the stealing, Malory, himself thief-turned-righteous, makes King Marc a brute from whom his chivalrous hero rescues the lady. The bliss of Joyous-Gard is interrupted when Tristram is called to war, and the story is left hanging there for three volumes, while Malory returns to the adventures of the other Round Table knights. In volume XII the author casually disposes of Tristram by killing him in a tournament. The last words of the dying lover are not, as Thomas wrote:

Amie Ysott, trez fez a dit,
A la quatre rent l'esprit . . .

Dear one, Iseut, three times he said,
And on the fourth his spirit fled.

No. According to Malory, Tristram's final farewell is: "Alas, my sword."

Malory's account, slotted somewhat casually into his Round Table collection, lacks lofty tragedy. In it, Tristan has none of the fresh force with which he burst upon the courts of Europe from the pens of earlier writers. All the same, by electing Tristan to Arthur's Round Table, Malory did much to fix him as an accepted figure of English, and later American, literature. Malory's Arthurian legend inspired generations. It was destined to live forever, and Tristan with it. Most of the writers who fell under Malory's spell associated Tristan closely with Arthur, but some were sufficiently intrigued by Tristan alone to delve into his past and resurrect the personality that had won the heart of medieval Europe—the young man for whom love was life and death.

FOUR

Sir Tristan
and the Troubadours

*The response to Tristan in medieval courts was a case of
the right story for the right audience at the right time.*
In fact, nobles and commoners alike in the 1100's and
1200's were in a mood to arch a bow, brandish a sword,
tackle a giant with Tristan, and ready to succumb to his
love potion. They were moved to pity by his anguish of
body and soul, unabashed to weep for his untimely
death. He was both their ideal and their entertainment.

So close was he to the heartbeat of the times that scholars who track trends in styles of the arts can't say whether the young knight set a fashion or was a supreme expression of it. In either event, in Tristan medieval society saw what it considered to be the flower of humanity. And society had the means to publish his deeds far and wide—the troubadours.

The troubadours were poets, a great majority of them from the South of France (those in the North were called *trouvères*), and in the year 1199 they were 466 strong. Five were kings, ten were counts, five were viscounts. Not a few were noble ladies. The remainder were mostly powerful barons, knights, or younger sons of high-born families who had been educated for the Church or for the fortunes of war, but preferred minstrelsy.

One, Guy Foulquey by name, became Pope Clement IV. As Pope, he had the habit of awarding indulgences—exemption from the penance usually required by the Church—to anyone who would recite his verses to the Virgin.

To be a troubadour was all the rage—but not everybody could compete. There were stiff requirements. First, the poet had to have talent; he needed an ear for rhyme and rhythm. Next, he had to accept discipline, to exercise his talent in accordance with precise rules

and regulations governing both the form and the sub-
stance of his poetry. A troubadour who became a popular favorite had reason to be proud of his mastery of the
art. The contest for acclaim was so severe that the win-
ners can perhaps be forgiven for challenging runners-up
in the words of the popular Raimbaut d'Orange:
*"Depuis qu'Adam mangea la pomme, il n'est pas un
trouveur dont le trouver vaille, auprès du mien, une
rave. Et si qu'el qu'un veut me démentir, qu'il revête
haubert, lance, écu, car je le réduirai par la defaite au
silence."* ("Since Adam ate the apple, there hasn't been
a single lyric poet whose verses—compared with
mine—are worth a turnip. And if someone wishes to
contradict me, let him arm himself with halbert, lance,
and shield, for I will bring him down into silence by
defeat.")

In the love lyrics of these master troubadours, Tristan
and Iseut were a constant point of reference. *"Mainten-
ant je sais que j'ai bu à la coupe ou but Tristan."*—Now
I know I have drunk of the goblet from which Tristan
drank. *"Les cheveux d'Iseut ne furent pas aussi beaux
que les cheveux de ma belle qui j'aime au feu de Tristan
amant."*—The hair of Iseut was not as beautiful as the
hair of my fair lady, whom I love with the fire of Tristan's love.

One of the most celebrated lyricists, Bernard de Ventadour, for a time enamored of Eleanor of Aquitaine and employed at her court, addressed to her these lines:

Plus trac, pena d'amor
De Tristan, l'amador
Qu'en sofri mainta dolor
Pour Izeut la blonda.

From love I suffer more
Even than, long before,
Tristan suffered for
Iseut the blonde.

Such were the popular comparisons that flowed from the quills of the troubadours.

The very first of the band was Eleanor's grandfather —friend of Breri—Guillaume, Count of Poitou, Duke of Aquitaine. Giant in stature, with long, blond, waving hair, a ruddy face, keen blue eyes, a ready smile, and a hearty laugh, Guillaume wrote poetry as robust as his person. His verses reflected his own love of good food, gracious women, and merry living. Not infrequently they were salted with humor, for Guillaume—a doughty fighter abroad—was an inveterate prankster at home.

One day, strolling along a roadside near his fields, he saw two women approaching on horseback with their handmaids. He discarded his rich outer doublet, disheveled his hair, and struck a beggar's pose, grunting like a mute dimwit. The ladies, whose husbands were away at war and were bored with a household devoid of males, took him home for their amusement. To make sure he really was a mute who would be unable to repeat castle gossip, they put an angry cat on his bare back. Count Guillaume continued only to grunt. After playing his role for a few days and garnering much savory gossip, he departed. From home he wrote the ladies a letter, signed with his name and title and sealed with his coat-of-arms, advising them to get rid of the cat.

Guillaume's verse lacked the gracenotes of the school of troubadouring which it founded, for the count was not a man for frills. These were added under the sponsorship of his granddaughter, Eleanor, to whom he left a heritage not only of vast lands—he owned more territory than the King of France—but of love of rhymes and rhythms. He left her too a sense of their fitness to convey the deepest feelings of the human heart.

Without Eleanor's sponsorship, it is quite possible that the troubadour school might never have reached the full flower which made it such a natural channel for the Tristan story. And certainly without Eleanor and her daughters Marie and Mathilde, such original Tristan authors as Thomas, Chrétien, Breri, and Eilhart would have had less encouragement.

Eleanor was also a patron of courtly love, an ideal which readied French audiences for a warm reception of Tristan and which Thomas used in the story itself, as a softening veil over the old tale's sharp Celtic contours.

This courtly love, *l'amour courtois*, was a fashion, but it was born of history rather than of whim. The twelfth and thirteenth centuries were times of the greatest crusades. The men of Europe were away for years at a time on these half-religious, half-avaricious ventures, and some never returned. Even at home, the lord of the castle was frequently off, warring with neighboring lords. The central monarchy was a weak instrument of government; the king, a mere chairman of his lords, each of whom was the autocrat of his own territory and the arbiter of his own boundaries. Each had to protect his own lands, and a good many had ambitions to annex the lands of others.

Consequently, the life of married women, like the pair whom Count Guillaume met by the roadside, was apt to be lonely. No one thought twice about woman's lonely lot, for the marriage relationship was considered merely a biological means to a political end, not a matter for the emotions. The end was purely and simply to produce heirs for landholdings and whenever possible to enlarge these holdings by uniting in marriage the heirs of big owners. In marriage, the partners were the machinery for the perpetuation and expansion of the power of the nobility.

Love . . . love was a different matter. It was to be had where it happened, and in love the partners were persons. So sharply were love and marriage differentiated that at one of the courts of love, traditionally held in the great halls of castles throughout the South of France, the lady judge and jury gave not only a go-ahead but a blessing to a petitioner who inquired whether it would be wrong for a divorced couple to have a love affair. The presiding judge, one Vicomptesse Ermengarde de Varbonne, a friend of Eleanor's, pronounced the opinion that such love would be an act of devotion in the highest sense, whereas in marriage it had been a sacrilege. Eleanor herself, wife successively of two kings and a pawn in the Norman ambition to rule all lands from Scotland to the Pyrenées, was confronted with a somewhat similar case at her court of love in her native Poitiers. The question turned on whether love and marriage could exist simultaneously. Her daughter Marie doubted it, but deferred to the greater wisdom of her mother. "I find it admirable," said Eleanor, "when a wife can find love and marriage consonant, but such a wife I have not yet met."

By contrast, the ideal of courtly love, which lady judges and jurors interpreted, was to the women of Eleanor's time what the ideal of marriage is to women today. It was perhaps even more compelling. *L'amour courtois* became a cult, second only to religion in its mystic importance in the life of the medieval woman of France, and to some extent of other countries as well. Perforce, it became important in the lives of the men around them.

Service of the ideal—called the service of love—

required four rituals to achieve a lady's favor: *le soupirant, le suppliant, l'amoureux, l'amant.* The soupirant
was the sighing wooer, the novice. The suppliant was
the wooer entreating on his knees. The amoureux was
blessed with the promise of his lady's love. Finally, the
amant was fully accepted into her graces. He was thereafter bound to perform her will as a vassal-knight was
bound to the lord from whom he had his lands and to
whom he swore loyal service. On the highest plane, the
amant responded to his adored one almost as a Christian
to the will of God. Woman's supremacy in courtly love
was perhaps a compensation for her defenselessness in
marriage. However, as her lover's goddess, she in turn
had her obligations. She was to be faithful, forgiving,
generous, gracious.

The testament of courtly love could be summed up in
the adoration of woman by man and the comfort of
man by woman. Passion was not part of the testament,
but in practice it was a natural accompaniment. The
love of Tristan for Iseut was the embodiment of the
ideal as practiced. Tristan's loyalty to Iseut above all
other loyalties, his belief that God sanctioned and protected their devotion, was fully in keeping with what an
educated audience of the time would expect of so noble
a knight.

In other ways, too, the romance reflected the beliefs
and manners of the courts it entertained. People took

literally the power of the magic potion the lovers quaffed. In the absence of science, superstition reigned. Even the well-educated believed not only in potions but also in trolls, dragons, dwarfs, and fate determined by the stars. The role of the evil dwarf who read the heavens to inform King Marc of the lovers' acts fell not as fantasy on medieval ears but as natural happenstance, as did Tristan's encounter with the maiden-eating dragon in Ireland.

To the medieval audience the description of the dawn trumpet-flares that shattered the lovers' nightly ecstasy in Tintagel's orchard had the familiarity that a shrilling alarm clock would have for the modern reader. And no doubt the same unpleasant associations! The trader of silks in whose likeness Kaherdin disguised himself when he brought Iseut to the dying Tristan was a familiar figure along every European coastline. Hauling holdsful of bolts of silk and brocade, ostrich feathers, pearls, spices, savory figs and dates, incense, ivory, and dyes, the trading vessels, black-sailed and white, cruised mostly from the Middle East, newly opened up by the Crusades. The merchant-sailors were the purveyors of textures, tastes, scents, sparkle, and color which livened the dungeon-like atmosphere of Europe's heavily fortified castles.

In every verse through which the story unfolds, rapt listeners recognized their own experiences, lifted and transmuted to heroic levels. Tristan's chivalry was the ethic of the day. To be brave in battle, to rescue women and the weak, to be courteous and generous—these were a knight's commandments. Often broken in actual life, they were all the more admired in Tristan.

King Marc's reluctant deference to his barons—else they could and would defy him—was the common embarrassment of kings. In the story this ignoble state of anarchy becomes soul-rending: Marc is torn between his love of his own nephew and his need to do the expedient if he is to keep his throne. The triumph of the feudal system is the instrument of Tristan's destruction.

The feudal system of government was, in essence, a jockeying for power between kings and the nobles who were supposedly their vassals, and between nobles themselves and *their* vassals. Life under this system was less high-flown in the living than in the reading, either then or now. A glimpse of medieval routine helps one to appreciate the spell of contrasting glamour which Tristan cast across the Continent and across the Channel.

The Middle Ages rested—none too securely—on three classes of society. On hill or cliff tops dwelt the nobility, with commanding views of the estates they owned, accessible by land or river. In the villages below huddled tradesmen and clerks; in the fields lived the peasant-farmers. All three classes shared in common a constant fear of attack.

Lords and villagers were walled and moated against marauders. Castle windows were not designed for enjoyment of the view. Mere slits, they were strategically placed as a means to sight from far off an enemy approach. Any invading cavalcade could be seen for miles, up or down river. On shore it had to wind along tortuous roads intended to make progress difficult and give the castle lord time to dispatch a routing expedition. If the expedition failed and the enemy neared the castle gates, then from the slit-windows, arrows could be zinged into his ranks. If some of the contingent managed a closer approach, a cascade of boiling oil descended from the slits onto their heads.

In the village the houses which modern tourists find so picturesque, pressed side to side and leaning over crooked streets, were to their original tenants dark, dank, and airless. Jammed together so as to economize on the length of the wall around them, they were infested with rats and vermin. The plague, a dread disease which rats and fleas transmit, wiped out whole villages at a clip.

The peasant, in his thatched cottage surrounded by fences of thorn for protection against wild animals, at least had air, even if he and his crops were totally at the mercy of war barons on the march.

War had no strategy. Its conduct bore no relationship to terrain. It was impossible to map campaigns because no one knew much geography, and few had ever seen or could read a map. In battle, knights lined up facing each other; behind them were their squires, who were learning to be knights. Charge! Then, hand-to-hand, the fighting began, a series of individual duels. Those beaten, if not killed, attempted to flee. Captives, often after being tortured, were thrown into deep castle dungeons, which they shared with rats and snakes.

A fourth group of men and women, the nuns and monks, lived outside the social structure in the limbo of their walled convents and monasteries. Usually they had not chosen the religious life but had been forced into it. They were the shipwrecks of society's disasters: the women whose husbands or lovers found them a drag on new ambitions, the sons whom fathers or rival heirs wanted out of the way. Some of the monks emerged as political advisers to aspiring power-grabbers, but never the nuns.

The nuns educated girls of noble birth who were sent to them to be made eligible for marriage. Wearing carved ivory alphabets on their belts like rosaries, convent pupils recited the letters like prayers as they strolled in arched and pillared cloisters, perhaps hungrily sniffing the good odors that came from the many fireplaces of the convent kitchen. They learned to read and write in Latin as well as in their own language. They learned arithmetic in the form of accounting; one day they must know how to keep castle accounts. They were taught to embroider, sew, spin, play the viol, sing, make medicine from herbs, ride horseback. All this they had to know by the age of thirteen or fourteen, when they were considered ready for barter to further their families' ambitions or bulwark their security.

Boys were taught at home. As soon as they could read, write, and figure, they were apprenticed to knights to learn how to bear arms and to hunt. By sixteen or seventeen, they had to be ready for knighthood. Sons of villagers were also apprenticed to masters of the trades they were to pursue—baker or swordmaker, vintner or goldsmith, woodcarver or weaver, or any of the dozens of small industries that supplied feudal needs. Often the boys learned to read, write, and keep accounts from wandering teachers who set up school wherever there were enough pupils, moving on when the supply dwindled. Sons of noblemen and villagers might meet at the universities, but for the girls of the village and for the peasants on the farms there was no education. Dreary drudgery—lugging the slop pails, tending the cattle, washing clothes in the streams, raising crops, grinding grain—was the lot of peasants or of village women.

On the farm, in convent, castle, and village, life was usually uncomfortable and often perilous, always uncertain, and frequently short. Death from war or disease lurked close to the living. It was into this atmosphere that the first family of Poitou introduced the patronage of writers, the excitement of the courts of love, and the refinements of troubadouring. This was the world throughout which the troubadours spread Tristan's fame. In this they were assisted by jongleurs, the minstrels whom troubadours engaged to recite their compositions. The troubadours created; the jongleurs repeated. Only before distinguished nobles, the equal of Eleanor's family, did troubadours personally perform. To the villages, on a holiday, or when a fair kept, the jongleurs brought Tristan and other tales and a repertoire of their sponsors' lilting lyrics. In castle halls of lesser nobles they were also welcome.

Picture a great hall where a court of love holds session. Here may be seen the touches of dignity and grace which were the gifts of Poitou, along with leavening luxuries from the Orient. In summer, the rushes on the floor are sweetened with roses, lilies, gladioli. In winter, rugs are laid. On the walls hang tapestries and silks from the East, embroidered in rose and blue by the ladies of the household. The walls, of buff limestone, have been plastered over and, where no tapestries hang, have been painted with flower designs, yellow, red, white, and gold. The curtains near the hooded fireplace have been drawn back; on that couch behind them the lord and lady will sleep when the curtains close again for night.

If there is occasion for celebration, dinner precedes the court session. A dozen tables have been laid, each with a fine cloth spread on top of the ordinary coarse cover. Gold and silver plates wrought by village artisans or looted from another castle replace everyday pottery. The knives, also silver and gold, are sharp, but there are no forks. Instead, the thumb, second, and third fingers, will be used. There are no napkins, but a bowl of water for rinsing hands is shared by every two guests. They wipe lips and fingers on the edge of the tablecloth. Beside every plate is a miniature, individual loaf of bread, baked with the barley, millet, or rye flour milled by peasants from the grain of the lord's fields.

The guests are seated. The women shut their ostrich-feather fans, square their brocade-slippered feet on the floor, stop talking and set to. They can eat as heartily as the men. The dishes keep coming: boar in clove sauce, venison in pepper sauce, booty with which the lord returned from the morning's hunt, his falcon perched on the cuff of the chamois glove the village tanner had fashioned for him. There are pies of pigeon and pheasant. When the pie crust is pierced, live birds escape. A page looses hawks to kill them. For dessert, servants deposit laden trays of cakes, tarts, dates, figs, and pomegranates. Watchfully they refill the goblets of spiced wine mixed with honey. At the end of the meal, mirrors are passed to the ladies, so that they may repair their makeup.

After the session of the court of love concludes its business of the evening, some guests may play chess or backgammon or roll dice. A jongleur or troubadour, depending on the rank of the hosts, may tell of Tristan. The party will have begun before sundown and it may end before an early moonrise, for tomorrow all must be up with the sound of the trumpets. After morning mass, to work. The host, briefly home, will be off to visit another baron with whom he is plotting an alliance against a third. Alone, his wife picks up the tapestry she is weaving. Perhaps she will draw the threads into a favorite tableau of the time, fresh in her mind from last night's recital: the scene at the fountain of the Tintagel orchard, with King Marc spying on the lovers from the branches of the great pine.

Part III

THE LEGEND TODAY

See you, friends? Do you not see?
How he shines ever higher,
star-surrounded, sparkling like fire?

From act II, scene III of
Tristan und Isolde *by Richard Wagner*

FIVE

Sir Tristan
of the Opera

---

*In the thirteenth and fourteenth centuries, troubadours
became the fashion in Germany. There these composers*
of love songs were called *Minnesänger,* from a German
word for love, *Minne,* and the German for singers,
Sänger. Gottfried von Strassburg gave up his clerking
for the bishop to join their ranks shortly after being
acclaimed for the Tristan which was to inspire the nineteenth-century composer, Richard Wagner.

But if anyone attending the first performance of

Wagner's *Tristan und Isolde* in the Munich Opera House on June 10, 1865, was familiar with Gottfried's Tristan, he would have found little resemblance between it and Wagner's. Wagner rewrote Gottfried completely, and from a completely different point of view. He cut the cast of main characters to six, whom he called, in German, Tristan, Isolde, Marke, Brangäne (Brangien), Kurwenal (Gorvenal), and Melot (an evil baron). He obliterated the other Iseut. What remained stage-front was a closeup of a triangle: a headstrong Isolde, a tortured Tristan, a noble-hearted Marke. In this intimate picture, Wagner could concentrate on his favorite operatic subject: human emotions. To these he gave free rein in words, music, and sometimes dance.

Like ancient Greek dramatists, he worked to create unity between music, action, and speech. He achieved it by tempo, key, tone, and composition of chords, mating these with mood. But above all he wove his web of unity with motifs. For each character he designed an individual melody or motif. These he repeated from beginning to end of the opera, embellished, speeded, slowed, softened, heightened, transposed—assigning them to different instruments and using them in whatever fashion he felt best expressed the emotions of his characters at any given moment. The form changed frequently, but the melody never.

In *Tristan und Isolde*, the lovers—who desire to be one, more than they desire life itself—logically share a single theme. Thus at the height of their bliss in their orchard rendezvous, a rapt Tristan can sing their melody with the words: "You have become Tristan, I, Isolde; no longer Tristan." And Isolde can reply: "You have become Isolde, I, Tristan, no longer Isolde." Then in duet:

Ohne Nennen, ohne Trennen,
neu' Erkennen, neu' Entbrennen
endlos, ewig, ein-bewusst
heiss erglühter Brust höchste Liebeslust!

Of names now shorn, partings gone,
newly born in fiery dawn
we share one soul forevermore
passion glowing at the core while we in ecstasy adore! *

Here their motif seems to take wings. It rises and falls, as a bird with the wind, and finally floats beyond hearing. Perfectly it conveys the illusion Wagner is trying to create in the scene: the souls of the lovers absorbed in the night.

The melody is first heard in the opening bars of the opera's overture. In pure form, it is the sound of yearning, like this:

---

* *German translations in this chapter convey the sense of the original without always using the same words. The preservation of rhyme, assonance and, where possible, rhythm, so important to the lyricism of the opera, has been given precedence over word-for-word literalness.*

In the first act, seconds before the lovers drink the potion, the motif issues a deadly warning, rolling ominous as a funeral march. As they quaff, it stings like a wasp. At other times the motif moans in anguish or exults in joy.

The first audience to listen to it did so with ears of stone. The opera offended the traditions of the day. Opera was supposed to be melodious and amusing. Tristan was dissonant and agonizing. Wagner was the first composer in musical history to use dissonant chords on a grand scale. Furthermore, he stripped his characters of the pretenses that were considered polite on the stage as well as in the drawing room and revealed Tristan and Iseut less as victims of a magic potion than as captives of their own instincts.

In the Wagner story Isolde, a vengeful vixen, attempts to give Tristan a *Todestrank*, death-drink, in return for his slaying of her Irish kinsman. In error, she takes from the hand of Brangäne the *Liebestrank*, love-drink. The fury of her pre-potion anger is then equalled by the fury of her post-potion love. However, the *Liebestrank* carries its own death sentence and the lovers soon come to desire death with all their hearts as the only possible release into a state, unattainable in life, of perpetual love.

At the instant when the lovers drink the fateful potion, Wagner, with his talent for dramatic unity, rolls love, hate, and death into a tremendous crescendo. The theme stings. The lovers stand stark still, staring as though seeing each other for the first time. Suddenly they burst into such a rapture of the theme song that they are oblivious to the simultaneous song of Marke's royal procession descending from Tintagel to meet them on Cornwall's shore.

In its medieval form, the legend might have appealed to nineteenth-century operagoers as a nice evening's theater, a romantic fantasy. Wagner's equation of hate, love, and death was harsh heresy. That first audience sat with its hands in its lap. Nor were those immediate witnesses alone in their horror. There was a general public outcry against Sir Tristan. Newspapers attacked him and Isolde. Priests preached against the lovers. "Tristan is buried," a desolate Wagner wrote to a friend.

Wagner had worked for six years to get his Tristan produced. He had tried in all the great cities of Europe—Paris, Berlin, Dresden, Vienna, among others—to find a sponsor who would pay singers, orchestra, opera-house rent, production costs. From time to time he had sneaked bits of the opera music into concerts. The bits were pronounced unplayable. Music critics warned him that his persistence could end his career. He persisted.

Finally he found a sponsor, King Ludwig II of the German state of Bavaria. At that point, the tenor chosen for the role of Tristan fell sick! When he recovered, the soprano selected to be Isolde became ill. Upon her recovery, rehearsals at long last commenced. The orchestra balked. The men were well paid and willing to follow their conductor as best they could, but they simply couldn't understand his dissonant work. Once Wagner literally stood on his head in his despair of ever getting them to master it. That they did so, eventually, is a tribute both to them and to the composer, for orchestras ever since have had trouble with the musical score of Tristan. It is among the world's most difficult scores to play well.

Why the stony rejection of Tristan in 1865? Where did the traditions that barricaded his first entry into the world of music come from? Ludwig II gives a clue in a letter to a young woman of his acquaintance. After the opera she had written him to urge that he break off his friendship with Wagner. In reply he wrote, "So it is from *Tristan und Isolde* that your aversion came. I can well understand that this creation might wound and repulse a pure, maidenly creature. How clever you are, Elizabeth. You compare my love for Wagner's music with my passion for the scent of jasmine, which latter you yourself struggle against in vain. There is something related in the two: sultry and intoxicating, the one as well as the other."

To understand why a proper young lady in 1865 should feel it necessary to struggle against the perfume of a flower, and equally dared not abandon herself to the enjoyment of eloquent music, it is necessary to know something of the times in which this young lady lived. She was a typical product of the Victorian Age.

For sixty-three of the years in the nineteenth century (and the first one in the twentieth), Queen Victoria sat firmly upon the throne of England and figuratively upon the social customs of the day. The regal lady cherished exceedingly straitlaced ideas about what should constitute the conduct and behavior of well-bred persons. The majority of her nine children and nineteen grandchildren married into the principal royal houses of Europe, carrying with them her standards of morality. Indeed, wherever Englishmen went in their expanding empire—for Victoria's was also the age of imperial conquest—the Victorian code went too.

It had rules for every situation—such as that no lady must ever be alone with a gentleman until and unless she became his wife. Victoria once wrote a long warning to an engaged granddaughter against going about with her fiancé without a chaperone. Commenting on a "want of delicacy" among certain youth who had violated this rule, the Queen let fall upon them the full acid of her scorn: "They are getting vy [very] American, I fear in their lives & ways."

Victorian etiquette reached into every nook of daily life, governing not only conduct but appearance. Women's clothing was dictated not merely by style but by modesty. "Limbs," the polite Victorian term for legs, had to remain covered at all times, even during active sports. The human body, its parts and processes, were subjects to be avoided in speech and cloaked from vision. Likewise, strong emotions were not to be displayed in public. Any well-born lady who defied this code was apt to find herself a social outcast. Moreover, the stigma would also include all her relatives. No wonder, then, that Ludwig's Elizabeth and her ilk in that first audience of Wagner's Tristan knew better than to succumb to the opera's candid unfolding of a passionate love.

But Victoria and her restrictions made for only half the trouble. Her century was also the century of Sigmund Freud. He was the Austrian physician who invented psychoanalysis, a method of helping people explore the very feelings Victorians struggled to hide. Freud felt that much mental illness was caused by overly severe repression of natural instincts, and he tried to show his patients how these natural instincts would out and, willy-nilly, influence their lives. He didn't publish these theories until very near the end of Victoria's reign and some years after the first disastrous presentation of Tristan. Nevertheless, products of the same period, Freud and Victoria offered their world two poles of opinion and between these poles personalities swung. The Queen and the physician were symbols of the emotional conflict prevalent in the nineteenth century.

Freud ferreted out and charted the relationships which Wagner sensed between love, hate, and death. Freudian definitions are technical; Wagner's are human. Freud was a scientist; Wagner, an artist. All the same, Wagner's Tristan and Isolde are perfect examples of what Freud defined as the "Eros instinct" (from *Eros*, the Greek god of love) and the "destructive instinct" in action. Freud could not have written Wagner's opera, but he could have predicted its outcome.

It was natural that Wagner should follow the pole of opinion Freud represented. He was himself a lifelong rebel. As a teen-ager he took a lively part in student riots. As a young man, he was active with political groups that wanted to form a united, democratic Germany, doing away with the separate states into which the country was then divided. He thought—and preached publicly—that German society needed shaking up from top to bottom, to make room for a new order which would allow for social and artistic freedom. He carried banners for that cause and was often found in the thick of armed scuffles with the police. Today he might be a young demonstrator at any European or American university.

Threatened with jail for his activities, Wagner later hid out in Switzerland, traveling with a passport faked for him by his dear friend, Franz Liszt, another great musician of the time, whose daughter, Cosima, later became Wagner's wife. During his exile in Zurich, Wagner had time to think about both politics and music. Watching the failure of the German riots, which had by this time mounted into a revolution, he came to the conclusion that violent physical revolt rarely produces reform but rather another, not necessarily a better, system. Musically, his reverie turned to Tristan. He conceived the idea for the opera at that time.

Exile tempered Wagner's political rebelliousness, but no adversity ever tempered his musical revolt. As a child, he had shown scant interest in the music lessons his family had forced him to take. Yet his stepfather, painter, actor, and dramatist, must have suspected his talent. Dying, the stepfather asked young Richard to play for him. When the boy had finished, the stepfather turned his head to his wife. "Could it be that he has a gift?" the dying man queried. But not until Wagner first heard Ludwig van Beethoven's "Symphony in A Sharp," did the gift stir within him. He was fourteen at the time. Twenty years later he could still vividly remember his reaction. "That one evening I heard a Beethoven symphony, I fell into a fever, became ill, and when I had recovered, became a musician."

Beethoven was his sole musical idol from the past. Once asked by Prince Albert, Queen Victoria's husband, to conduct a series of Beethoven concerts in London, Wagner gave his first concert without using a score. The critics took offense and criticized him severely. For the next symphony, a score rested on his conductor's stand. The critics praised his performance to the skies. Wagner then announced that the score on the stand had been that of *The Barber of Seville*—an entirely different composition by an entirely different composer—and that furthermore it had been upside down!

His work habits were as individualistic as his theories. He liked to wear silk clothing while composing in a well-furnished, carpeted room. He enjoyed having Robber, his Great Dane, with him, and the dog often stretched out under the piano. Wagner worked with intensity, but he hated the bother of putting neatly on paper the profusion of notes that rang in his mind. He once wrote to Liszt: "Can't you tell me of someone who would be capable of transposing my rough pencil sketches into a clean score? This clean-copying uses me up!" Mathilde Wesendonk, a friend who heard of this aversion, sent the composer a gold pen, which seemed to make the task of notation more pleasant.

Weather also affected Wagner's creativity. During the time he was putting down the score for Tristan, he wrote to Mathilde: "When the air is clear and fresh, I am ready for anything, just as when I am with one who loves me; but when the atmosphere oppresses me, I feel cross and contrary and things beautiful are hard to realize." He sought, most of all, spontaneity in his work, but at the same time he knew that spontaneity could not be sought; it had to come of itself. "I know it, this spontaneity in writing Tristan, and there is no happiness superior to it," he told Mathilde as he progressed with the opera.

At least part of the score was probably written in Hohenschwangau, a tiny, Alp-sheltered castle on a bluff overlooking the Bavarian village of Schwangau. The name of the village means "place of the swan," and Hohenschwangau is the high place of the swan, symbol of the nobles who ruled this part of Germany in the Middle Ages.

The castle still stands. Like all Hohenschwangau's rooms, Wagner's was richly appointed, with its white-enameled, gilded piano and carved mahogany four-poster bed. The ceiling is gilded with scroll work, the walls glow with murals, and the carving above the arched oaken doors is fit for a cathedral. Certainly, here Wagner had the luxury in which he claimed he could do his best work.

And if he wanted a breath of his favorite clear, fresh air, he had only to open the casement window. He could look up to the Alps, snow-dressed in winter, silvery brown and gray in summer while still capped with snow at the peaks. He could look down to the Alpsee, the deep little lake, color of sapphire, which the mountains cradle. If he worked late, the lake might be moonlit. Then, in its three-hundred-foot depths, he could see the moon six times reflected, depth after depth, in the water. He could see the lower, forested mountains reflected black, and the snowy peaks above reflected charcoal. Dark and still along the shore would be the towering pines. Still. So still he could hear the splash of a jumping fish. Below him the moonlight would fall on the fountains of the castle courtyard. When at last he drew the casement shut, could there not have been an overflow of inspiration for the night-song under the pine by the fountain in the orchard?

In Wagner's time, the castle belonged to Maximillian II, King of Bavaria, and later to Maximillian's son, Ludwig II, who made possible the production of the Tristan opera. Ludwig carried his interest in Wagner to an extent which could have provoked serious trouble had not Wagner handled it with great diplomacy. Fifteen days after he was crowned, the nineteen-year-old monarch sent a servant hunting for the composer, with a note offering to make it financially possible for Wagner to do anything he pleased, write what and how he wanted, and have all his needs attended to. There was just one condition: Wagner must stay close to the boy monarch's side.

The messenger, bearing the royal ring as proof of the legitimacy of this somewhat astonishing invitation, found Wagner living in poverty and more than ready to accept. Wagner not only moved into Hohenschwangau, but brought with him many friends from the music world, Liszt among them. Ludwig hadn't bargained for the friends, but he put up with them. What he really wanted was to have Wagner all to himself. He was fascinated not only with the music but with the personality of the man. It soon became apparent that the fascination was not healthy.

The truth is that Ludwig was mentally ill. Living in a world of daydreams and flinching from contact with his own world, he imagined himself to be a knight of the medieval world, like those in Wagnerian opera. On a pinnacle-shaped crag within sight of Hohenschwangau, he built another and far more elaborate castle, Neuschwanstein, New Swan Rock. This he fancied as the castle in Wagner's opera *Lohengrin*, where the Holy Grail, the cup used at Christ's Last Supper, was guarded.

Inside, the walls were muraled, floor to ceiling, with scenes from all the Wagnerian operas that had been produced when it was built. The Tristan murals the King reserved for his own bedroom. In crimson, sapphire, emerald, gold, bronze, rose and petal pink, they tell the lovers' story from beginning to end. The love scene in Tintagel's orchard spreads across the wall above the King's bed.

The castle has a dream quality, like a stage set, both inside and out. It is many-turreted, creamy white. From its balconies, one looks down on the red-roofed village of Schwangau, the miniature castle of Hohenschwangau, and the sparkling Alpsee. Just below is the misty waterfall which Ludwig, for all his impracticality, found a way to harness for running water in the castle. On the fourth floor a singers' hall duplicates the great halls in which the troubadours and minnesänger of the Middle Ages competed for royal favor. Today Wagner concerts are held in this hall. Its ceiling beams rest on columns topped with carved bears and fabulous unicorns, dragons, devils, angels. So gleaming is the floor that crown-shaped chandeliers, twinkling from the ceiling, are reflected in its parquet oak.

Ludwig's throne room is two stories high. Blue and green columns, rising from floor mosaics of deer and peacocks, support a balcony around all four walls. The room is reached by a spiral staircase, from the landing of which a plaster palm tree grows, its branches brushing a ceiling shimmering with stars.

The people of Bavaria were castle-minded; they didn't object to the astronomical cost of this monument to Wagner, but the court and the royal treasurer did. Both court and people objected strenuously to Ludwig's fanatic attachment to Wagner himself. In strong terms they petitioned the King to send him away. Ludwig proposed to abdicate instead. Tactfully, Wagner persuaded him to do no such thing. He left the royal presence. Thereafter, the two men saw little of each other. Once Ludwig arranged a secret meeting in the dead of night; several times he attended performances, incognito, in the Wagnerian opera house in Bayreuth, which he gave the composer the equivalent of $200,000 to help build.

On June 10, 1886, Ludwig was declared officially insane. Three days later he drowned. Whether his death was suicide or murder is not clear; his peculiarities had made powerful enemies. Wagner had died three years earlier of heart failure as he stood up from a long session at his piano. His devoted dog, Robber, died shortly afterward and was buried by his side in Bayreuth.

Many Wagner music lovers besides Ludwig helped build the Bayreuth *Festspielhaus*—festival storyhouse—as it is called. Shares of stock in the venture were bought by Wagner societies. During his lifetime,

Wagner himself gave to the building fund the proceeds from many concerts. The result was a red-brick monstrosity on the outside, but inside, a beautifully designed theater for Wagner's purposes. Since the first performance in 1872, Wagner festivals have been held every year in Bayreuth, with the exception of the years between 1945 and 1951.

It wasn't easy to get the Bayreuth project underway. Today a Wagner festival commands an international audience and the name Bayreuth means Wagner to music lovers round the world. But in Wagner's day, few people outside of Bavaria had ever heard of the sleepy little village.

Bayreuth was the fulfillment of Wagner's loftiest dreams. He regarded it almost as a temple and refused to allow applause at the operas performed there. This rule no longer holds, but out of respect for it the singers don't take curtain calls, so as not to prolong the clapping.

After Wagner's death, his wife Cosima ran the festivals. The management stayed in the family. In more modern times, Wagner's grandsons, Wieland and Wolfgang, took over. After Wieland's death, Wolfgang brought in other artists to assist him.

In 1952 and 1962, Wieland was responsible for two of the greatest productions of *Tristan und Isolde* the music world has ever applauded. To prepare for them, he went to Cornwall, visited the Fowey ruins, and pondered over the inscription on the Cunomorus stone. He wandered through mythical Tintagel, steeped himself in the Celtic lore on which the legend is based, and then he turned to Freud, reading deeply for psychological interpretations. The result: a streamlining of the drama's setting. Wieland stripped it of the gaudy scenery of grand-style opera, leaving the stage to the souls of the lovers. They seemed to bare their emotions in eerie light against stark and scanty props, suggesting now a ship's prow, now a castle parapet.

Imagine the reaction of an audience seeing the 1952 production for the first time. Anticipating a novel evening, 1,344 music lovers file through the ten doors, five to a side, that open into the amphitheater. Men and women in fashionable evening dress fill the rows of seats which curve, aisleless, across the entire Festspielhaus. Some couples climb to the balcony. Others sit in the royal boxes once occupied by kings, queens, and emperors. One large family is seated in the box where Ludwig, his cloak wrapped about him for anonymity, once brooded over the themes in Wagner's music.

The lights halfway up the columns surrounding the hall dim and die, then the lights at roof level. The tiny lights on the musicians' stands in the orchestra pit twinkle like subterranean stars. The pit lies so deep below the stage that the orchestra calls it "the abyss."

The familiar yearning theme sighs into the dark. The overture swells to its climax, fades, ceases. The curtain parts. A spotlight singles out an elliptical disk, surrounded by a dusky but translucent curtain. From within the curtained disk, Isolde's voice rises, high, clear, arrogant, wild. "Where are we?" she demands of her handmaid. "Air, Air! My heart suffocates within me." She throws back the curtain, revealing behind her the outlines of a ship's prow and gunwale. The light broadens, blues, to make the stage seem a sea. The illusion of a voyage to Cornwall has been created.

After the first act, if the night is fine, the audience strolls out to the terrace surrounding the Festspielhaus. There is less chatter than usual. The spectators feel shaken. They had expected the new, but not the startling. Now they are not sure what to expect next.

What they see when they return is again the disk. A bench has been placed upon it. This is the Tintagel orchard. When the lovers meet on the bench, the lighting makes them seem to float on a dark velvet cloud. They melt into Wagner's night of love. But when King Marke approaches, the velvet web is ripped away. The stage is bright, garish day. A grave, majestic Marke, compassionate while aggrieved, sobs out his bafflement at Tristan's betrayal of his trust. A penitent Tristan, broken by the anguish of his uncle gives Isolde an invitation to the eternal night of death:

Wohin nun Tristan scheidet,
willst du, Isold', ihm folgen?
Dem Land das Tristan meint
der Sonne Licht nicht scheint:
Es ist das dunkel nächt'ge Land . . .

Where Tristan now goes forth
will't thou, Isolde, follow?
In the land that Tristan means
no shaft of sunlight ever gleams;
It is the land of utter night. . . .

And Isolde accepts:

Wo Tristans Haus und Heim, da kehr' Isolde ein. . . .

To Tristan's house and home, there shall Isolde come. . . .

Now all dissonance fades from the lovers' theme. It becomes one of resignation. Tranquilly, the melody transcends all previous heights.

Suddenly it is interrupted by Melot, the baron who has led Marke to the lovers. In a series of chromatics, scales using all the sharps and flats on the staff, Tristan lashes into savage anger. His frustrated love erupts into hate. "Defend yourself!" He turns on Melot. Swords clash. Tristan is wounded.

In the third act, the disk supports a bier on which Tristan is dying. Cubes in the background suggest his castle in Kareol (the Lyonesse of Wagner) to which

Kurwenal has transported his wounded master. For the audience, the set has a larger significance. The lighting has turned it into the semblance of a wasteland.

Isolde is on her way to him. "Tristan!" the audience hears her call. Tristan gasps out his last breath in an effort to reach her. On that final breath, the theme is carried, piercingly sweet, with an undertone of the sting that sounded in the potion scene. The theme throbs with anguish as Isolde sings to her lover's corpse. It echoes in the lament of Marke, who arrives too late to free the lovers for each other in life. They have already accepted the freedom of death. Erect at the edge of the disk, Isolde sings her swan song, the final aria of the opera. In this, her *Liebestod*—love death, as the aria is called—she sees Tristan among the stars, shining like one of them. Her voice soars with her spirit to meet him and the theme reaches an even higher pitch than in Act II when she accepts his invitation to death. Muted thunder rumbles. The disk seems to move into the infinity to which the lovers now belong. The curtain descends.

The audience is filled with emotion. In some eyes there are tears. Not until later, over the supper tables at nearby restaurants where singers and audience gather, does the debate over Wieland's staging begin. The debate stimulated Wieland to review his concepts. Ten years later he modified them, using broader lighting effects and introducing more Celtic shapes, like the ship's prow—this time in the form of columns, and some with circular openings. He brought back onstage the chorus, sailors, and courtiers, whom he had previously banished to the wings. He mellowed, but did not embellish, his previous production. This 1962 Tristan, repeated in 1966 and again in 1968, after his death, was Wieland's victory. It won him the hearts of his audience, the universal acclaim of critics, and a special niche in the history of musical interpreters of Tristan.

The conductor who worked with Wieland Wagner was Karl Böhm, a stocky, gray-haired, studious-looking man who had learned as a youth the difficult art of conducting this and other Wagnerian pieces from a master conductor of Wagner music: Richard Georg Strauss. Strauss had been one of the first of the Festspielhaus conductors after Wagner himself. At sixty-eight, Böhm's age at the time of the 1962 performance, he was himself a master.

A Böhm rehearsal of Tristan illustrates the difficulties which even the most skilled musicians have with the opera's tricky tempos and nerve-shuddering tones. Listen for a minute to Böhm at work with his orchestra in the abyss, in the empty Festspielhaus. It is the beginning of Act III. Tristan, Kurwenal, and a shepherd are on stage.

"No, no," Böhm says. "The A-flat. It is A-flat! A-*flat!* Do you see, first violins, do you see? Right there, the eleventh bar, where you come in on an A."

"But don't go slower. We stay in tempo. Yes."

"No, no! *Too* early, that third beat. That must be exactly with me or we'll not all be there together."

He looks up to the singers, corrects a word in a line the shepherd sings. "Check text," he says. "You'll see I'm right. And you came in just a fraction late."

To the violins again: "Sh, sh, gentlemen, it is pianissimo [very soft] after all. Otherwise we can't hear Tristan up there." To Tristan: "Mark it, dear friend, it's clear for tonight." Marking is a beating through of the rhythm of a singer's lines, so as to save his voice for the actual performance.

At noon, orchestra and singers break. The rehearsals, even final ones, are rugged, but unlike the earliest performers of Tristan, at least these artists can relax to the extent of being sure of the reception their work will earn them.

In Spoleto, Italy, in July 1968, a quite different group of artists gathered to produce Tristan. The occasion was the Tenth Annual Spoleto Festival, founded by the Italian composer Gian-Carlo Menotti. Menotti's own operas are all distinctly modern; perhaps the one best known to young people is the tender Christmas story of *Amahl and the Night Visitors*. Menotti's interpretation of Tristan was in some ways even more modern than that of Wieland Wagner. "Wagner with Perfume," some of the critics headlined their comments, referring to Menotti's use of perfume in the orchard scene. He had it sprayed into the audience! Shades of Ludwig, Elizabeth, and jasmine. "The 'tryst' is back in Tristan," commented *Time* magazine, describing the abandon of the love scene and the youthfulness of the singers.

One of the problems with operatic Tristans has been that only mature stars, with long experience, can sing the difficult music. It demands breath as well as skill, and long breath requires a deep chest. Middle-aged, barrel-chested performers haven't looked much like the teen-agers Tristan and Isolde were supposed to be. Wagner himself once told a friend that the only way to get the most from the opera was to take off his glasses and listen.

Menotti decided to change all this. For Isolde he picked a graceful American ex-chorus girl, Klara Barlow. For Tristan he chose an ex-Marine, Claude Heater. Both had had some—but not extensive— operatic experience. During the orchard scene a ravishing Barlow and a handsome Heater, scantily clothed, sank to the grass, following minutely Menotti's coaching. "Love!" he had shouted at them during rehearsal. "Love—Love! Pure ecstasy!" He was not concerned with Wagner's psychological insights. What he wanted to project was a youthful surrender of body and soul to an all-consuming love. He got the effect he was after from staging and acting—but not from the music. His stars lacked the voice power of the famous Tristans and

Isoldes of the past. Nor was it easy for them to project what power they had while lying down!

The Spoleto Festival is handled in the opposite fashion from the Bayreuth Festival, where months of careful planning and weeks of rehearsal precede performances. Menotti is casual in his approach to programming. The programs are subject to sudden changes; they usually start late. Tristan happened to start half an hour early. The orchestra, composed of men who had never played the score before, had had only four days to rehearse. Their timing was off, their tones impure. Isolde had a cold. The curtain caught fire during the second act.

Though many critics ridiculed the performance, others praised Menotti's courage in attempting to bring *Tristan und Isolde* into harmony with the present day. The opera has, after all, been controversial from its birth. The nature of the controversy shifts as techniques of interpretation change. The significant fact is that for more than a century the opera has continued to inspire new approaches. There seems to be a lure within Wagner's musical retelling of Gottfried's legend that succeeding generations of musicians have not been able to resist. Each projects upon it the spotlight of his own understanding, a spotlight colored—as was Wagner's original conception—by the mood of the age in which he lives. And so Sir Tristan of the opera wears an iridescent cloak.

Sir Tristan
and the English Poets

Richard Wagner wasn't the only artist of Victorian times to train a spotlight on Sir Tristan. In England the young knight starred in three epic poems: one by an Oxford University professor of poetry, Matthew Arnold, another by Queen Victoria's favorite lyricist, Alfred Lord Tennyson, and a third by the romantic poet of that age, Algernon Charles Swinburne. After publication of these poems, between 1852 and 1882, the Wagner opera was revived in London—fortunately just

in time for the composer to see his masterpiece succeed.
In 1886, three years after his death, the opera won
thunderous applause in New York City. In music and
rhyme, Sir Tristan was charging toward the twentieth
century.

Nor was he in Victoria's day a stranger to lovers of
English literature. He had already been revived in the
reign of Queen Elizabeth I and again toward the end of
the eighteenth century. In 1596, the Elizabethan poet
Sir Edmund Spenser made Tristan a hero in his epic,
The Faerie Queene, a Maloryesque account of virtuous
knights at the court of Queene Gloriana of Faerie Land.
Gloriana was a glamorized Elizabeth I. Elizabeth was
charmed with her portrait in verse and ordered her royal
treasurer to reward Spenser with one hundred pounds.

"That is too much," objected the treasurer.

"Then give him what is reason," replied Elizabeth.

The treasurer interpreted this concession according to
his own lights: he gave Spenser nothing. After a few
months, Spenser dispatched to the Queen this message:

I was promised on a time
To have a reason for my rhyme;
From that time unto this season,
I received nor rhyme nor reason.

The Queen reinstated her original order for a hundred
pounds and saw that it was carried out.

In Canto II of *The Sixte Booke of the Faerie Queene,* *contayning the Legend of Sir Calidore, or Courtoisie,* Tristram is a promising young squire apprenticed to Sir Calidore to learn the arts of knighthood, especially the rules of courteous behavior. He rescues a lady in distress in a forest. What feats he may later have accomplished, we don't know, for half of Spenser's manuscript—including the rest of Tristram's story—has disappeared. The castle in Ireland where Spenser lived during most of the time he was writing *The Faerie Queene* was burned in an uprising against the British. The missing portion of the manuscript is thought to have burned with it.

For the Tristan legend, the burning was no loss. Spenser used it purely to convey a message: the importance of training young people in the practice of high ideals. No portion of *The Faerie Queene* is noted for lively characters or exciting action. Music is the poem's distinction. Spenser invented a nine-line stanza, held together by three and only three recurrent rhymes. The first eight lines contained five beats each; the last line, six. This form can be very graceful, but also very demanding. To keep within it, Spenser was sometimes forced into such absurd contortions as: "But since it me concerned myself to clere." Or, "There him he caused to kneele and made to sweare . . ."

Oddly enough, Spenser's dull Tristram served as an

inspiration for a lively, swashbuckling Tristrem by Sir Walter Scott some two hundred years later. *The Faerie Queene* was well thumbed by that Scottish novelist and poet whose lifetime spanned the end of the eighteenth and the beginning of the nineteenth centuries.

As a child, Scott delighted in reading. He had plenty of time for it, being often sick. At the age of two, he had polio. Doctors then knew very little about his disease and it was diagnosed as "teething fever." Without proper treatment, the disease left him lame for life. Later he was subject to chest hemorrhages, probably caused by tuberculosis. Confined to bed for months on end, he read and read and read. His favorite stories came from medieval literature and Scottish folklore. Out of his knowledge of them, as well as his interest in Spenser's *Faerie Queen*, came his own *Sir Tristrem*.

Scott's family were the descendants of an old and distinguished Scottish clan. The boy felt a mystic connection with the mythology of the wild Scottish Highlands. After he had recovered from the worst of his illnesses, he was sent to recuperate on his grandfather's estate in the heart of Highland country. He absorbed tale after tale from his grandfather's shepherds, with whom he liked to wander, sometimes sleeping with the flock in remote pastures. Later he made it his business to collect systematically the shepherds' folklore. He became expert in translating the dialects in which it had been set down.

The first part of his *Sir Tristrem* is a reconstruction of a manuscript dating from about 1230 in one such dialect. The rest is Scott's own invention, written in a precise imitation of the original language. Scott came across the manuscript in the musty stacks of the library of the law school of the University of Edinburgh, his college. He was convinced that his find was the work of Thomas of Erceldoune, an early thirteenth-century Scottish poet, reputed also to be a prophet. Scott wrote a preface for his *Tristrem*, almost as long as the poem itself, setting forth his theory. Poem and preface were published in 1804. Scott's scholarship came more from the heart than the head and was later disproved. The manuscript was one of the Tristan tales that abounded in the British Isles in the early thirteenth century, but it wasn't written by the prophetic Erceldoune.

Though Scott's scholarship was dubious, his poetry was good. In terse ballad form, his story of Tristrem and Ysonde, as he calls the pair, stands out in Celtic starkness. Here is an example:

*Nighen woukes and mare,,
   The mariners flet on flode,
Til anker hem brast and are,
   And storms him bestode;

In reading, pronounce all final e's as separate syllables. For instance, in line 1: woek-es and mare-e.

Her sorwen and her care;
   Thai witt that frely fode;
Thai nisten how to fare
   The waves were so wode
      with winde;
O land thai would he yede,
If thai wist ani to finde.

In the modern prose translation which Scott provided to help readers over the hurdle of the old dialect, he tells us that this stanza describes the plight of the boy Tristrem's kidnappers. For more than nine weeks the ship is wracked by storm. Anchor and oars are lost. Food supplies dwindle. The waves are so wild with wind that the sailors cannot control the boat. Believing the tempest is their punishment for the kidnapping, they long to put Tristrem on land, if only land can be sighted. Some stanzas later, Tristrem is finally beached at the foot of Tintagel's cliff.

From there on, the original thirteenth-century author, and after him, Scott, gave the legend some novel twists. At one point Ysonde goes off with an old beau from Ireland. Tristrem lures her back by playing the harp. Tristrem's death-dealing wound is inflicted in a battle during which he is defending a younger Tristrem, a lad much like Spenser's squire, from the onslaught of fifteen bandits. Tristrem spares the life of the bandits' leader after extracting from him a promise to build a hall and people it with statues retelling the story of Tristrem's devotion to Ysonde. There is more fighting than lovemaking in the tale; it is more of an adventure story than a romance, with clannish feuds in the Highlands undertoning the clash of medieval swords.

This element of derring-do stamped all Scott's work. In contrast to his own physical disabilities, he made most of his heroes strong physical specimens. He also made them master strategists, perhaps in imitation of the gift for strategy with which he himself made up for other deficiencies. As a grade-school student competing for the reward which accompanied the top position in class, he made it his business to observe carefully the habits of the single rival who stood between him and his goal. He noticed that whenever the other boy was called on to recite, he fingered a certain button on his jacket. One day Scott secretly snipped the button off. The rival fingered frantically, looked down for the missing button, and forgot what he had intended to say. During that recitation Scott surpassed his competitor.

Later in life, his shift from poetry, his first love in writing, to prose novels was also a matter of strategy. The star of another poet of the time, George Gordon, Lord Byron, began to rise a few years after Scott published his *Tristrem*. Recognizing Byron's genius and his own inability to compete with it in verse, he turned to the novel as the best means of maintaining his popularity.

It may well be that Scott told the Tristrem–Ysonde story to his children, as he often told them the plots of his novels and poems. Sometimes he would spin a story out for a day as he rode horseback with the youngsters over the hills and fields of Abbotsford, the large estate he had bought with his earnings. He had personally drawn the plans for the remodeled castle in which the family lived, and it was dear to all their hearts. On days too chill for riding, he sometimes gathered the children near the great fireplace in his library for the storytelling session. Above their heads were arrayed shelf after shelf of blue, leatherbound volumes, glowing softly in the firelight. Each volume was stamped with a portcullis, the grilled-iron barrier gate of medieval castles. These were Scott's own works. Across the room ghostly faces seemed to flicker in the stained-glass windows. They were the faces of the Scottish kings that Scott had scattered in jeweled panes throughout the castle. Perhaps a gypsy or two might linger in the doorway, listening. On the top floor of the castle, the big attic was always open as free lodging for gypsy troupes and for poets and actors who had fallen on hard times. It was the kind of household, this Abottsford, in which a Tristan bard could feel at home.

In later life, Scott's prosperity vanished. He owned an interest in the companies that published and printed his work. The firms went broke. Thereafter Scott worked furiously to pay off his share of the debts. He wrote,

wrote, wrote, sometimes not stopping to eat or sleep for forty-eight hours at a stretch. He paid off every cent he owed, but the superhuman effort killed him.

Scott's *Sir Tristrem* was written more than a quarter of a century before Victoria became Queen. To him, there was no conflict between the essence of the tale and what was then considered the essence of good taste. Probably there would have been none, even later, since Scott was so little concerned with the love relationship of his characters. But the narrative poets who next adopted Tristan—Tennyson, Arnold, and Swinburne— were primarily concerned with human emotions. The Victorian conflict between the way people felt and the way they felt they must act hit each of the three poets hard. Each solved the conflict in his own fashion, and the solutions make their accounts of the lovers into very different stories.

Matthew Arnold's solution was to attempt compromise. The passion of the old legend lives in his retelling, but in order to make it acceptable to the sensibilities of his readers, Arnold gives the heroine's role to Iseult of Brittany, respectably married to Sir Tristram. She is fair and pure:

Our snowdrop by the Atlantic Sea,
Iseult of Brittany.

By contrast he presents Iseult of Cornwall as a raven-haired siren, as evil as she is beautiful. He tries to dispose of her attraction by settling Tristram down with the snowdrop and giving the couple two children. We have a glimpse of the infants sleeping "on the castle's southern side" in a room in which the moon "shines upon the blank white walls and on the snowy pillow falls." But Arnold is unable to maintain this picture of innocence and domesticity. His compromise breaks down before the irresistible Iseult of Cornwall, evil or no, and before the surge of Tristram's desire for her.

Actually, Arnold begins his poem on this note of truth. In the first scene, Tristram is dying and hoping for Iseult's arrival before death.

"Is she not come? The messenger was sure.
Prop me upon the pillows once again!
Raise me, my page! This cannot long endure.

Christ, what a night! how the sleet whips the pane!
What will those lights out northward be?"

His page replies:

"The lanterns of the fishing boats at sea."

And Tristram, seeing the snowdrop by the fireplace:

"Soft, who is that stands by the dying fire?
Ah! Not the Iseult I desire!"

From this point on, as Arnold relates the earlier events which have led up to this death scene, he engages in a losing struggle to hang on to his compromise. As in these opening lines, he uses throughout a special gift: accentuating the mood of his characters with the quality of the weather. In the last scene, as Iseult of Cornwall dies with her lover,

The air of the December night
Steals coldly round the chamber bright,
Where those lifeless lovers be.

Up to the last moment, Arnold keeps fighting. He tries to punish Iseult of Cornwall, when she comes to Tristram's deathbed, by showing her as a wasted creature, her beauty gone. The result is that she emerges a resplendent figure of tragedy, aware of her loss of youth and capable of saying that when the snowdrop looks upon her, she may well cry:

". . . Is this the foe I dreaded?"

The lovers die as one, and in exasperation the defeated author exclaims to his readers:

It angers me to see
How this fool passion gulls men potently.

Arnold's *Tristram and Iseult* is of special interest for two reasons. The first is the tug-of-war between the

author and his characters. Reading the poem, one is
newly awed by the undiminished power of the old
legend to shake a man's soul—even against his will.
Second, Arnold was the first poet to give the Breton
Iseut a distinct personality. In previous accounts, she
had been mainly an obstruction in the way of the lovers'
destined pursuit of passion. Arnold makes of her much
more than a proper Victorian wife. She has a quality of
wistfulness which is at once winning and heartrending.
The poet takes us to her a year after Tristram's death.
She is standing among holly trees, watching her children
play. "Joy has not found her, nor ever will," Arnold
admits. "She seems one dying in a mask of youth."

And now she will go home and softly lay
Her laughing children in their beds and play
Awhile with them before they sleep, and then
She'll light her silver lamp, which fishermen
Dragging their nets through the rough waves afar
Along this iron coast, know like a star.

In the lamplight she sits embroidering, occasionally pat-
ting Tristram's dog. At midnight, she prays; then to
bed, thinking:

. . . and tomorrow'll be
Today's exact repeated effigy.

It is believed that this Breton mother was modeled on a

real personality: Arnold's first love, identified in some of his other poems as Margaret or Marguerite. We don't know why he never married her. The marriage Arnold finally made worked out well enough and he was devoted to his children, but his poetry is always at its best in the recollection of impossible love.

He began writing when he was thirteen and won several prizes for his poems at Rugby School, where his father was headmaster. He also won a reputation as a cutup, sometimes delighting his fellow students by standing behind his father's chair and punctuating the headmaster's earnest admonitions with grimaces and irreverent gestures. Anything but a model student, he preferred fishing to homework. Later his father became a history professor at Oxford University and Matthew followed him as a professor of poetry. By then he had become interested in the arts and in current events. He had grown into a big, black-haired, handsome man, with a taste for loving and living, as well as a talent for verse and for the critical essays to which he later turned. In these he lashed mercilessly at the social and economic repressions of his times.

The seesaw between the proper and the true that marks his Tristram was to some extent characteristic of his life. Not so with Alfred Lord Tennyson. In all his poetry and all his life, Tennyson chose conformity. Tennyson's Tristram is a handsome but thoroughly unlovable blackguard. His Isolds (as he calls the Iseuts) are lifeless as puppets. Tristram takes advantage of both women simultaneously. His death is the price of his sin. He is about to kiss the Cornish Isold's throat, having stroked the locks which Tennyson, like Arnold, dyes black, when:

Behind him rose a shadow and a shriek—
"Mark's way," said Mark, and clove him through the brain.

The tale of Tristram, called "The Last Tournament," comes near the end of Tennyson's *Idylls of the King*, Round Table stories based on Malory, and, like Malory, using the Arthurian cycle as a warning against the consequences of unrighteousness. But whereas Malory was capable of lyricism (and so, in some of his other works, was Tennyson), "The Last Tournament" reads like a blank-verse sermon—and not very rhythmic blank verse at that. Not the slightest breath of emotion warms the lines. Often their avoidance of feeling reduces them to the ludicrous. At a moment when the reader is led to believe that Tristram is about to make love to Isold, he suddenly announces, "Come, I am hunger'd," and demands meat and wine!

Tennyson's inspiration for the *Idylls* began in childhood. He read Malory avidly, and he and his seven brothers used to play at holding Arthurian tournaments. Four sisters acted as the ladies to defend whose honor the brothers whacked away with wooden swords. At the age of eight, Tennyson started writing his own adventure stories. Sure that his minister father would not approve of the stories, he kept them hidden under some rarely used vegetable dishes in the kitchen cabinet. Sometimes the Tennyson children acted out these stories too; often Alfred read them aloud to the others when all were supposed to be asleep at night.

The Arthurian legend had a hold on his imagination. As a mature poet, he hiked all through its Cornish setting, frequently rambling over the ramparts of Tintagel. He traveled to Brittany to visit spots associated with Arthur and with the Tristan tale. He steeped his mind in both Arthurian and Tristan lore, but it never seemed to seep into his heart. His defenses against emotion were, unlike Arnold's, as impregnable as the castle walls he was fond of describing.

His defenses were also deep-seated. Despite his childhood fancies of adventure, Tennyson soon became a proper Victorian. He decried Cambridge University, where he studied for a while, as "a villainous chaos of din and drunkenness." When his father died, he had to leave the university for financial reasons, but apparently he didn't regret the leave-taking. Offered an opportunity to return, he refused. While there, he entered and won a poetry contest. The poem he submitted was an old one, but he shrewdly judged that it was the right selection to win the cash prize. It was the cash—not the proof of excellence in his art—that interested him. He planned to arrive on top, some way, somehow. As a boy, he told one of his brothers, "I mean to be famous."

Understandably, he wanted to escape the poverty and difficult family life which wrecked his teens. His parents didn't get along with each other. One brother went mad and had to spend the rest of his life in an institution. Another brother was addicted to drugs. When Tennyson did indeed arrive, it was with a sour view of the unorthodox and a determination to hang on to what he had achieved by playing it safe.

His disciplined pen and a gift for flowing verse earned him both financial security and social position. He bought an elaborate country estate, "Freshwater," on the Isle of Wight, off England's southern coast. Queen Victoria made him her poet laureate, charged with celebrating official occasions in verse. Newspapers referred to him as "the state oracle."

Tennyson opposed anything that might threaten that comfortable position. He fought reforms that would give the vote to all citizens, not merely to the rich, whose exclusive privilege it was at the time. He was against laws to improve working conditions for factory laborers. He wanted to keep everything just as it was. He was strictly "Establishment." Nothing he ever wrote would have shocked Ludwig's maidenly Elizabeth as Wagner's Tristan did. Tennyson chose the opposite pole from Wagner.

Algernon Charles Swinburne *would* have shocked Elizabeth. He called the Victorian era, into which he was born in 1837, "this ghastly, thin-faced time of ours." At Oxford University, where the first part of his *Tristram of Lyonesse* was written, he made friends with the painter-poet, Dante Gabriel Rossetti; the designer and writer, William Morris; and others of the Pre-Raphaelite school. The Pre-Raphaelites were so-called because they looked for inspiration to Italian artists who had preceded the famous painter Raphael and who were noted for the natural poses of their subjects, especially their nudes. The English Pre-Raphaelites were dedicated to the search for truth in art. They were in full revolt against the artificialities of the Victorian age.

The first part of Swinburne's *Tristram*, like all his work prior to 1879, reflects Pre-Raphaelite aims. The poet had long loved the Tristan legend and had spent many hours discussing it with his Oxford friends. When Tennyson's "The Last Tournament" was published, Swinburne was anguished. He felt that Tennyson had cheapened the nobility of the old tale and had degraded its primitive beauty. His ambition to write his own version was spurred.

By the time he was thirty, Swinburne had become the rage of artistic London—that is, of the section of it that was beginning to defy the Victorian code. He was an unattractive man, tiny of body, huge of head, with hair described not merely as red but as orange. His magnetism was in his speech. He talked as he wrote, with a fluent and extremely lyric vocabulary. His large eyes roved restlessly around the group to which he talked, shining with the earnestness of his convictions. The lashes which he fluttered frequently were so long that he complained they tangled in the wind.

Swinburne particularly enjoyed reading his own work aloud and hardly had to be invited to do so before whipping his newest manuscript from his pocket. As a child, he often recited the poetry which he was even then writing, to his friends, as they cantered along on their horses. He also wrote blood-curdling dramas in which everybody was stabbed to death before the play ended. These he and his cousins used to perform together. His cousins found his company a perpetual adventure. His adult personality was equally exciting to London's literary vanguard.

Perhaps too much hero worship or too many parties went to his head. Or perhaps something troubled him that was not apparent in his rambunctious outer behavior. In any event, he took to drinking so much that he lost track of what he was doing, where he was, or what he had done with his work. He left a considerable portion of his *Tristram* in a taxicab and later had to write it all over again. In 1879, Swinburne's mother asked the family lawyer, one Walter Theodore Watts-Duncan, who also dabbled in poetry, to take Swinburne into his home and look after him. The lawyer cured the poet of drinking. He also monitored all his writing, guiding it away from the Pre-Raphaelites and into Victorian conformity. He progressively robbed Swinburne of the very talent he had been assigned to rescue. Of all Swinburne's work after 1879, his *Tristram* was the least damaged. By a series of devices, probably instinctive, Swinburne managed the feat which Arnold could not, of appearing to bow to Victorianism while actually mocking it.

For example, in the beginning his Breton Iseult is introduced as a model of Victorian propriety. At her first meeting with Tristram:

She looked on him and loved him, but being young
Made shamefastness a seal upon her tongue,
And on her heart that none might hear its cry
Set the sweet signet of humility.

But as the poem progresses, Swinburne rips away this shroud of gentility and reveals the hellcat in Iseult's breast. From the moment when she discovers that she is not Tristram's true love, she lives for one purpose only: revenge. Her life becomes one long scheme for getting even. Spun of infinite hatred, her scheming is concealed behind the behavior of the perfect wife. It is in her private prayers that we hear her ask God:

"Shalt thou not put him in my hand one day
whom I so loved, to spare not, but to slay?
Make me thy sword. . . ."

She nurses Tristram with seeming devotion during his
last illness; actually she is exulting at nearing her goal.
Knowing that Tristram, calling deliriously for his own
Iseult, is beyond hearing *her*, she speaks—indeed, almost
hisses forth—her mind. The bedside scene is an antiphony
of Tristram's longing and her hatred. The two speak
alternately, Tristram saying:

"For more than watersprings to shadeless sands
More to me were the comfort of her hands. . . .
More to my sense than fire to dead cold air
The wind and light and odor of her hair. . . .
More to my soul than summer's to the south,
The mute, clear music of her amorous mouth. . . .
Iseult, Iseult, what grace hath life to give
More than we twain have had of life, and live?
Iseult, Iseult, what grace may death not keep
As sweet for us to win of death and sleep?"

And the Breton Iseult replies:

"Fear not but death shall come."

Then as the ship bearing the Irish Iseult finally
approaches shore, white-sailed, the sweet wife tells her
husband the sail is black. In that moment:

The white maiden laughed at heart. . . .
And scarce with lips at all apart
Spake and as fire between them was her breath;
Yea, now thou liest not, for I am death. . . .
And darkness closed as iron around his head
And smitten through the heart, Tristram lay dead.

Swinburne had a masterly command of the art of making two themes play a duet throughout a scene, sometimes, as at Tristram's death-bed, to create contrast, other times to create harmony. The most dramatic example in *Tristram of Lyonesse* is a scene in which the Irish Iseult, alone in her chamber in Tintagel, prays the night through that God will forgive Tristram for the sin of loving her, another's wife. The scene also illustrates the deviltry with which, in this poem, Swinburne was able to outwit his censor, Watts-Duncan. The prayer spoken to the tune of a storm raging outside the castle would seem to be a piece of proper Victorian penitence. But hear it through. As Iseult kneels:

. . . the Eastwind girded up his godlike strength
And hurled in hard against the high-towered hold
The fleeces of the flock that knows no fold,
The rent white shreds of shattering storm.

The storm gathers strength as Iseult's prayer becomes more agonized. God rides in the storm and He is neither a tender God nor a forgiving one, but rather a remote and vengeful deity who can be satisfied only by the sacrifice of flesh and blood. Iseult offers herself as the sacrifice:

"Let *me* die rather, and only; let me be
Hated of him, so he be loved of thee."

And as a full field charging was the sea
And as the cry of slain men was the wind.

Appealing still further, Iseult asks of God:

"Know'st no more as in this life's sharp span
What pain thou had'st on earth, what pain has man?"

And like a world's cry shuddering was the wind
And like a God's voice threatening was the sea.

Finally, in utter selflessness which is in sharp contrast to the other Iseult's selfish prayers for vengeance, the Irish Iseult cries:

". . . Yet be thou
God, merciful, nay show but justice now.
. . . And be this
The price for him, the atonement this, that I
With all the sin upon me live and die."

She has given up asking for mercy—"nay show but justice"—and her offer to lay down life, body and soul, for the salvation of her beloved is apparently accepted:

Like man's heart relenting sighed the wind
And as God's wrath subsiding sank the sea.

A shaft of dawn light streaks through a high-slit
window. Exhausted, Iseult throws her arms around
Tristram's dog.

And all her heart went out in tears and he
Laid his kind head along her bended knee.

Watts-Duncan must have been completely baffled to see
the confession of sin on which he had insisted turn into
a means to ennoble the sinner, degrade the virtuous, and
expose the Victorian god as a most un-Christian tyrant.

The sound of the sea which crashes to a crescendo in
this scene swells throughout Swinburne's poem, and the
look of it flashes from every page. The poet was a sea
lover and, in spite of his tiny, almost misshapen figure, a
tremendously strong swimmer. He once swam at the
base of Tintagel's cliff, successfully battling the angry
waves which batter the resistant rock. He got a
banged-up leg from the battle, which kept him on
crutches for three weeks but didn't diminish his delight
in his victory. To a friend he wrote: "You can't imagine
how the sea . . . beats and baffles itself against the steep
faces of rock . . . It was queer, dark gray, swollen water,
caught, as it were in a trap and heaving with rage
against both sides at once, edged with long panting lines
of incessant foam that swung . . . along the deep, steep

cliffs without breaking and had not room to roll at ease."

In his *Tristram*, this shore became

The beachless cliff that in the sheer sea dips,
The sleepless shore, inexorable to ships.

And through the poem's Tintagel a "tidal tune" rings ever from the sea. His Irish Iseult is "more fair than the sea's foam"; his Breton Iseult muses at sunset until

... the fire in sea and sky
Sank and the northwest wind spake harsh on high
And like the sea's heart waxed her heart that heard,
Strong, dark and bitter ...

His dying Tristram sighs:

"What rest may we take ever, what have we
Had ever more of peace than has the sea?"

And finally, the sea washes even over the lovers' graves:

For many a fathom, gleams and moves and moans
The tide that sweeps above their coffined bones. . . .
And over them, while life and death shall be,
The light and sound and darkness of the sea.

The greatest of all the poem's sea scenes, however, is Tristram swimming. Here Swinburne gives free rein to his own sensations of delight in the water:

Toward the foam he bent and forward smote,
Laughing, and launched his body like a boat,
Full to the sea-breach, and against the tide. . . .
And mightier grew the joy to meet full-faced,
Each wave and mount with upward plunge and taste
The rapture of its rolling strength and cross
Its flickering crown of snows that flash and toss
Like plumes in battle's blithest charge, and thence
To match the next with yet more strenuous sense. . . .

Swinburne drew from many sources in writing his
poem, and the story combines them all, not always logically. Its glory is in the poet's magic with words, his
character portraits of the two Iseults, and his ability to
capture the quickening pulse of passion as the story
unfolds. On the voyage from Ireland to Tintagel, the
lovers' "four lips became one burning mouth." As the
vessel approaches shore, they stand—

Soul-satisfied, their eyes made great and bright
With all the love of all the livelong night.

Later, in their forest sanctuary

Each hung on each with panting lips and felt
Sense into sense and spirit melt

Whether they are together or apart, in love or in longing, the beat of the pulse mounts steadily until the
couple dies, "with love for lamp to light us out of life."

Like Swinburne, Thomas Hardy, the next English poet to take over the legend, rejected Victorian prudishness. Unlike Swinburne, he utilized no tricks in presenting his tale of passion. He didn't even bother to throw the Victorians a sop. The two men were contemporaries and neighbors for part of their lives, but they barely knew each other. Hardy was a social hermit, as sparing of speech as Swinburne was verbose, having a conviction, mirrored in all his writing, that tragedy is man's destiny. The Tristan tragedy was a natural subject for him and one that appealed to him for nearly half a century. A deliberate man, Hardy took that long to decide to tackle it.

Hardy's *Famous Tragedy of the Queen of Cornwall at Tintagel in Lyonesse* is a one-act play in verse. It was written for what we today call "community theater"—that is, production by amateur companies. We would also call it "theater in the round," for Hardy directed that it be presented without scenery in a drawing room. The drawing room, he says in introductory instructions to the players, "is presumed to be the Great Hall of Tintagel."

He dedicated the playlet to "those with whom I spent many hours at the scene of the tradition." Like other English writers who were attracted by the old story, he had as a youth clambered over Tintagel's cliffs, once spending the better part of the night under the stars there with the girl he courted and married. He knew the cliffs intimately, in fine weather and foul. His cast of characters includes a chorus of "shades of dead old Cornish men and shades of dead old Cornish women." Their lines intensify a mood of deepening doom, with all the feeling of Tintagel on a cold, gray day when a storm is brewing.

Hardy doesn't follow any of the medieval versions of the story. He merely uses them to build a brand-new story of his own. He begins with a Queen Iseult newly returned to Tintagel from Brittany. Iseult of the White Hands, married to Tristram, has sent for her raven-haired rival because her sick husband is moaning for his true love. However, when the black-haired beauty arrives, Iseult of the White Hands has second thoughts and announces that Tristram is already dead. He isn't, but his wife, looking on her rival's beauty, cannot bring herself to admit her to Tristram's presence.

This background is related in conversation between Queen Iseult and her handmaiden, Brangwain. The conversation is interrupted by a messenger bringing news that Tristram is alive and recovered from his sickness and on his way to Tintagel. The messenger has hardly time to make his exit before a harper arrives, who is, of course, Tristram in disguise. The harper sings to Iseult, his lyric setting forth a plan for the two to meet that night:

"O living lute, O lily rose,
O form of fantasie,
When torches waste and warders doze,
Steal to the stars with me.

While nodding knights carouse at meat
And shepherds shamble home,
We'll cleave in close embracements, sweet
As honey in the comb."

Next on stage is the blond Iseult of the White Hands,
who has pursued her errant husband. She begs the
Queen to take her on as bond-wench, so that she can at
least be near Tristram. But Tristram will have none of
this.

. . . "I never more can be
Your bed-mate, never again,"

he announces and orders her home. To no avail; she
hangs on to the bitter end. The Queen forgives Tristram
his marriage because she accepts as a fact of life that:

A woman's heart has room for one alone,
A man's for two or three.

Now enter King Mark, who sees through Tristram's disguise. He stabs Tristram, whereupon Queen Iseult stabs
Mark and jumps from the Tintagel cliff to the sea. Tristram's dog jumps with her. Iseult of the White Hands is

alone in the drafty castle (or the drawing room). With
a shudder, she wails:

"This stronghold moans with woes
And jibbering voices join with wind and waves
To make a dolorous din."

The chorus takes over as she finally departs for home.

The melodrama is saved from sounding like an invention of kindergarteners by the shivery sense of a
haunted place into which Hardy's way with words
turns the drawing room. One can believe that the spectators watching the first production by the Hardy Players, in Dorchester on the evening of November 28,
1923, had an interesting hour. The form was new for
that time, and its imagery cast a spell in the old grange
hall chosen for the presentation. The spell was intensi-
fied when the lines of the chorus were later set to music.
Hardy was a novelist and something of a poet. He was
distinctly not a playwright. Nevertheless, his exercise in
community theater adds to the variety of forms in
which Sir Tristan lives on.

At 8:15 p.m. at the Century Theatre in London, on
Monday, February 21, 1927, Sir Tristan again appeared
on stage, this time in a full-length verse play by John
Masefield, soon to be appointed Britain's poet laureate.
Unlike the acclaim which Tennyson's appointment as
royal rhymer received, the choice of Masefield by King

George V evoked an outcry of protest. It wasn't Masefield's subject matter that was provocative—Victorian
regulations over such matters had crumbled two decades
before—but the man's style. It didn't seem like poetry
to those who associated that art with flowery language
and romantic imagery.

Masefield was a down-to-earth poet. He liked to picture people as they were and to put on their tongues the
kind of speech they would normally use. He wrote long
narrative poems, as well as verse plays, in which the dialogue was always modern and often rang with the slang
of the streets and the sea, for Masefield knew both well.
At seventeen he had run away to sea, later tended bar in
a tough neighborhood of New York City, and worked
for a while in a carpet factory in the New York suburb
of Yonkers. Returning home, he began his writing
career as a newspaper reporter, covering day-by-day
events. He never lost the good reporter's thirst for truth
and disdain for frills. And so his *Tristan and Isolt*, like
all his poetry, is terse and forthright. His aim, he said,
was to make "poetry a school of life, instead of a school
of artifice."

The characters speak with honest simplicity. Isolt,
instead of trying to hide her love for Tristan, tells her
husband outright: "I love him so that I am all his to the
spirit." Later, repentant, and returning to Marc from
her love life with Tristan in the forest, she admits her
shame as frankly as she earlier avowed her love:

"... I have sinned in act and in thought,
Broken all vows, all pacts; tricked you, betrayed you.
Now, touched to loyalty by the greatness in you,
I stand ashamed ..."

Marc replies:

"Isolt, my Queen, we have been harsh to each other."

Then Isolt, with the wry wit that often illumines a scene:

"You do not know my worst."

All the love scenes are entirely natural. "Look, darling—you know as I do that we are each other's," Tristan remarks, taking Isolt in his arms.

Underlying this twentieth-century impression is a skillfully woven fabric of the old sources, which Masefield had painstakingly studied. The Welsh saga appealed to him and he played it up more than any other Tristan author since the Middle Ages. From the saga comes the pig-stealing episode which Masefield turns into an hilarious bit of theater, using it to make fools of the evil barons who conspire against Sir Tristan. The knight has asked Hog, King Marc's swineherd, to take a message to Isolt at a summer castle. Hog would like to be helpful, but he is in a predicament. King Marc has promised him freedom from serfdom if he manages to prevent the theft of any pigs for a year. Tristan's request comes on the last night of that year. Hog dare not leave the herd untended. So Tristan offers to guard the pigs himself.

Evil barons get wind of the plot and plan to attack Tristan in the pigpen, expose him, and steal a pig. Of course Tristan is too clever for them. The barons strip in order not to soil their fine clothes in the mud and filth of the sty. Tristan catches them and takes them, dirty, naked, and shivering, to Marc. They stand before him, his supposedly trusty courtiers, caught—more than bare-handed—trying to steal his pigs.

Along with folklore Masefield mingled history. With a reporter's persistence, he had searched for the real identity of the legendary characters. In his play, Tristan is a Pictish prince. Arthur is a general. Marc is a very military king. Isolt is a part-Norse princess. The giant whom Tristan slays is one of the Norse pirates who conquered Ireland in the eighth century. He has forced a noble Irishwoman to marry him and Isolt is their daughter. Having promised the dying giant to bring her to King Marc, Tristan sails to Ireland. When he and Isolt meet, it is love at first sight. The potion is incidental. They drink it as a toast to their love, from a shell brought fresh from the sea. Thereafter the story follows the French medieval pattern, with some omissions—such as a second Iseult.

Toward the end, the plot becomes pure Masefield. Marc dies at war. The widowed Isolt becomes Queen of Cornwall, ruling with dignity, wisdom, and grace. In the course of the play, Masefield has let life hone her from a headstrong lass to a superb stateswoman. Her growth, through love and sorrow, is the heart of the drama. Masefield shows Isolt not merely as a vision of beauty but as a woman of character. Yet neither does he desert the core of the original legend. The power of Isolt's constant love for Tristan draws her finally to the forest where he lies, half crazed and dying for the love of her. As she arrives, he whispers a limpid Masefield translation from Thomas:

"Isolt my blood, Isolt my breath,
In you my life, in you my death."

And Isolt, her work in Cornwall done, replies: "I will come with you, Tristan." Arthur finds the dead pair and buries them, "spirits of love," together.

The outstanding quality of the Masefield play is its credibility. Having chosen the excerpts from legend that suited him, and having reconciled them with history, Masefield transposed them into modern English and let the characters do the talking. There are no asides—as in so many earlier versions, including the medieval—of either pity or condemnation, no editorializing. The story is high-grade reporting on events leading inevitably to doom, yet without omitting the lighterhearted flashes which are also some part of any life, no matter how tragic its ending. Masefield's treatment of the lovers ushered them into the age of modern communication.

Sir Tristan
Comes to America

"I came down here with the intention of writing some short things for a new book, but our old friend, Tristram, whom I have been fighting off for some five years, got me finally by the throat and refused to let me go. Just what I shall do with him or what he will do with me is more than I can say yet, but it is evident that he won't let go of me until one of us is finished."

The year of that contest was 1925, the place an artists' and writers' summer colony at Peterborough, New

Hampshire, and the writer of these words the American poet, Edwin Arlington Robinson. Finishing his letter to his friend, Robinson turned to his writing pad, tore off a page onto which he had crammed ninety lines of blank verse—written very lightly, so as not to bear down on his pencil—and added the page to a pile of five others, written with a similarly frugal regard for wasting neither paper nor lead. The five contained 550 lines of verse, a week's work.

Almost a year later, back at Peterborough, Robinson wrote to the same friend: "Yesterday I killed Tristram and Isolt in an experimental sort of way."

The experiment didn't turn out to suit him and he tried again. And again. He spent the summer killing them. By early autumn he was satisfied. In September 1926, fourteen months after he had succumbed to Tristram's grip on his throat, Robinson finished a 4,493-line narrative poem, called, simply, *Tristram*.

On the surface, it would seem that Robinson was the most unlikely man in the world to write a throbbing love story. This tightly reserved New Englander, born in Maine, with the typical reticence of the Down Easter, had also all the deep-seated New England dislike of emotional display. *Tristram* was entirely different from anything he had ever written before. "The key and color of this thing may cause some readers to suspect that I'm getting a little tired of hearing about my New

England reticence," the author commented. And he added: "Which may be pretty true."

Tristram was also entirely different from anything Robinson would ever write again. Instantly, it met with a popular success he was never able to repeat. This one-time wonder landed high on the best-seller list, a rarity for poetry, and in the first year after publication was reprinted seventeen times, six times within the first four months. "More, more," his publishers and public begged, but the poet did not have it in him to oblige. Whatever there was of passion in his soul, the legend had ignited, then utterly burned.

Already respected as a superfine craftsman, Robinson had twice won the Pulitzer Prize. *Tristram* brought him this honor for the third time. *Tristram* also brought him something he had never known in his life: wealth. The poet used it to buy many things he had been forced to forego for lack of money, especially clothing and books, but he lacked the self-indulgence to buy luxuries, except cigars. He gave to charity a great deal of what *Tristram* earned. He did try to hire expert typists, but his habitual thrift with pencil and paper made his manuscripts so hard to decipher that good typists were reluctant to tackle them—even for the best of money!

Invitations to accept honorary degrees from universities, to be guest of honor at parties, to give readings from *Tristram* at fantastic fees poured across his desk.

He refused them, every one. "I like my friends; people are another matter," he said. But he was saddened that Harvard, from which he had graduated as a younger man and where he had been happy and stimulated, didn't see fit to offer him an honorary degree. He would have accepted that.

At Harvard, he and a group of friends had formed the Corncob Club. Meetings were given over to reading, then discussing, poetry. Robinson had been writing poetry since he was eight years old. The retreat where his childish verses were composed was a barn on the farm where his family lived, in Gardiner, Maine. Sometimes young Win, as he was called, curled up in the hayloft to write; sometimes he crawled into a sleigh. More often, he turned an old oatbin upside down and used it for a desk.

The barn was his retreat from his considerably older brothers, who often beat him, and from parents too preoccupied with their own problems to care. The quality of Robinson's childhood comes clear in a confession he later made: he thought the Bible quotation that he learned in Sunday school, "Suffer the little children," meant that children were born to suffer. So unwanted had been his arrival that his parents didn't even bother to name him. When he was six months old, summer visitors in Gardiner, boarding with relatives of his mother, put several names in a hat and held a drawing. The name drawn was Edwin. The person who drew it came from Arlington, Massachusetts, so Arlington was added as the boy's middle name. Young Win knew this story; it was a town joke.

His mother was a vague and helpless woman; his father lazy, loud-voiced, ill-tempered, and frequently drunk. Finally the father washed his hands of reality and fled to spiritualism. The family's dilapidated farmhouse rattled all day long and into the night with noises his father claimed were the clamor of the dead. Books slid from shelves, dishes from cupboards—the mischief of the old man's saucy spirits. At meals the senior Robinson would sometimes make the whole table rise from the floor without apparent mechanical devices. Professing to have supernatural powers, he devoted his last years entirely to this sort of conjuration. In fact, the family was a seedy lot, a pitiful petering-out of a long line of sturdy Maine shipbuilders and seafaring folk.

Only Edwin rose above this environment. Both brothers grew up as shiftless as their father; one became a dope addict and alcoholic. The poet supported them, and their wives and children, all his life. His nieces and nephews adored him. He liked a good romp with them. Afterward he would bring out his violin and fiddle tunes for them.

Robinson related well to children, but he was always standoffish with adults. His childhood had left deep scar tissue, and few were permitted to know him well. He never married. Good friends, both men and women, came to appreciate his mind; everyone who met him admired his gentleness and kindness. But no one save he himself—and perhaps not even he—knew his heart.

His only clear passion was his poetry. In *Tristram*, Robinson abandoned himself to this passion as never before or after, working with an impetuous intensity which was abnormal for him. Before surrendering to Tristram's grip, he had studied much Celtic and Arthurian lore, but his previous poems based on it had, in his own words, "refrigerated the critics."

He had also read all the Victorian versions of the Tristan legend. Understandably for his personality, he found Swinburne hard to take. The bad writing in Tennyson offended his standards of craftsmanship. Matthew Arnold he liked wholeheartedly. Robinson's Breton Isolt owes considerable inspiration to Arnold's wistful and winsome Breton girl, to whom Robinson added womanly dimension. His poem opens as she stands on a rocky coast. She

Could see no longer northward anywhere
A picture more alive or less familiar
Than a blank ocean and some white birds
Flying and always flying and still flying,
Yet never bringing any news of him.

The poem ends with her, after Tristram's death, again with the birds and the sea:

Alone with her white face and gray eyes,
She watched them there till even her thoughts were white
And there was nothing alive but white birds flying
Flying and always flying and still flying,
And the white sunlight flashing on the sea.

Between these scenes, the story unfolds largely in conversation among the characters. The plot, mainly from
Malory, introduces not only Arthur, but other knights
of the Round Table, especially the fickle-hearted Sir
Gawaine, for a time in love with the Breton Isolt. Ladies
of Arthur's court also play roles, including Arthur's fey
sister, Morgan, who is hopelessly in love with Tristram.

But these other loves are subplots, a kind of ornamen-
tation of the central love affair, like the illumination of
a parchment scroll. The focus remains on Tristram and
the Irish Isolt. There is no love potion. Robinson
expressed deep scorn for this device: "Men and women
can make enough trouble for themselves without being
denatured and turned into rabbits." And so the poet's
lovers fall neither magically nor suddenly—but rather,
gradually and naturally—in love; first Isolt with Tristram, later he with her. Robinson doesn't think much of
Mark; he uses him to get in a few digs at marriage,
referring to Isolt as

... the bartered prey
Of an unholy sacrifice, by
Rites of Rome made holy ...

But something in Mark eludes Robinson's scorn. In the end the King emerges with dignity and compassion, saying to Isolt:

"I shall do no more harm to either of you
Hereafter, and cannot do more to myself."

He tells her the banished Tristram is free to return to her.

". . . All I ask
Is that I shall not see him."

When the returned Tristram is murdered by an evil baron, Mark strangles the baron.

Mark's Isolt is black-haired and violet-eyed. Isolt of Brittany is fair-haired, gray-eyed. The former is desire walking; the latter, "half child-like and half womanly," is "frail," "light," and "mysteriously strong." To her adoring father she seems "like a changeling down from one of those white stars." Robinson makes her seem born to suffer in a world in which she does not belong and endows her with the patience to bear the pain of her destiny and the charity to hope that there are not many women "or many of them to be" who are so destined.

The poet is at his best in conveying the quality of her suffering and in conveying, by contrast, the joy of Tristram and the other Isolt in their sojourn at Sir Lancelot's castle of Joyous Gard. "You are the stars when they all sing together," Tristram tells Isolt as they make love. The morning after, he tingles with life "and the green grass was music as he walked." Even here, however, the lovers have the foreboding that their love will be short-lived.

"We are not for the fireside or for old age
In any retreat of ancient stateliness.
If that were so, then this would not be so,"

Isolt says. And adds:

"Mine is a light that will go out sometime,
Tristram. I am not going to be old.
There is a little watchman in my heart
Who is always telling me what time it is."

But no matter.

    . . . Years are not life,
Years are the shells of life, and empty shells
When they hold only days and days and days.

And below them, as the lovers clasped each other,

A measured sea that always on the sand . . .
Poured slowly its unceasing sound of doom
Unceasing and unheard and still unheard.

The sea washes all through the poem. But, unlike Swinburne's many-mooded sea, Robinson's is the grim, monotonously threatening sea of the Maine coast. It is "a changeless moan"; it is "cold waves foaming on the rocks below"; it is "a warning and a torture . . ."

Like a malign reproof reiterating
In vain its cold and only sound of doom.

Robinson's poem was published almost simultaneously with the first production of Masefield's play. Neither poet knew the other or knew that the other was at work on the same theme. Some little-known American poets had preceded Robinson in writing about Tristan, as some lesser lights had preceded Masefield, but the public on either side of the Atlantic Ocean hardly knew that these pieces had been published. Neither did Masefield offer Robinson any competition on the Atlantic's western shores. Robinson's version won America easily.

Of course, Wagner's opera had already introduced the tale to Americans, and the opera has to this day remained one of the best-loved among audiences that attend performances at America's opera center, the Metropolitan Opera House in New York. The popularity of Robinson's love story was a hit not merely in New York and other big cities, however, but throughout the country. It was read in farmhouses, schoolrooms, on trains and buses, at club meetings, on the beach in summer, by the family fireside in winter. The slim, wine-colored volume was everywhere to be seen—by the bedside table, in women's handbags, at the lunch counter, in the glove compartment of the car. The name Tristram was everywhere to be heard on everybody's tongue. Lending libraries had waiting lists for the volume. Bookstores couldn't keep it in stock. The darling of the Middle Ages had become the rage of the world's most modern nation.

In writing the love poem, Robinson exhausted himself not only creatively but physically. He was never really well afterward, although his death, of cancer, did not come until nine years later.

After Robinson's death, the world seemed almost content with the number of ways it could recall Sir Tristan. As the twentieth century moved on, only one other author, again an Englishman, gave readers any really new light on the old tale. A brief but highly original treatment, partly in dialogue, partly in narrative verse, appeared in 1941. This poem, *The Death of Tristram*, was the work of Robert Laurence Binyon, curator of Oriental prints and drawings at the British Museum.

Binyon begins with the dying Tristram, who refuses to believe that the sail of Isoult's ship is black. He drags himself from bed, staggers to the castle parapet, sees the white sail, and

A voice that empties all the earth and sky
Comes clear across the water, "It is I!"

He struggles to stay alive while Isoult, having landed, struggles to climb to the parapet. She makes it—he is alive—and in the moments remaining to them, they reminisce, their conversation evoking the memory of their romance. Binyon returns to narrative to describe their death in each other's arms. Isoult of the White Hands finds them thus. She has their bodies richly robed and sent to Cornwall where Mark, lamenting, receives the funeral ship.

The distinction of Binyon's poem is that it breathes as much with the tragedy of Mark and Isoult of the White Hands as with that of Tristram and the Irish Isoult. The curator-poet gives us a moving record of the grief of the Cornish King and the Breton wife. As the vessel bearing the dead lovers leaves the Breton shore, Isoult of the White Hands says:

"Farewell, my lord, thy home is far from here,
Farewell, my great love, dead and doubly dear.
Carry him hence, proud Queen, for he is thine,
Not mine, not mine, not mine."

And Mark, receiving the bodies in Cornwall, echoes her as he gazes at the corpse of his Queen:

"And now the end is come, alone I stand,
And the hand that lies in thine is not my hand."

Binyon wasn't a newcomer to rhyme and rhythm when he wrote these lines. His verses had won him a prize at Oxford University and he had continued to write after his graduation. His close friends were a distinguished group of English poets who, between World Wars I and II, accomplished the difficult feat of smoothly combining realism and romanticism. *The Death of Tristram* is a skillful example of this combination. As such, it deserves to come out from under the shadow of the many other versions among which today's reader can choose.

In the last three decades of the twentieth century, will still another Sir Tristan take men's hearts? It is now seven or eight hundred years since he first stormed the courts of medieval Europe, making strong men blink and set their lips and women weep. These courts were as sophisticated for their time as our society is for ours. The troubadours who sang Sir Tristan's fame knew well that only the genuine, only the finely styled, could win them the favors to which, penniless, they aspired. They calculated well in choosing Sir Tristan as a subject. He could win them the hearty meals of venison and boar, the wine and honey, the warm, fur-lined capes, the steed to ride, the bed, silk-curtained, in the castle tower. Sir Tristan won the modern equivalent of these comforts for the unwanted child from Maine, named from a hat, who became Edwin Arlington Robinson. And though it was not desire for luxury but rather the force of inner compulsion that drove Robinson to let Tristan wear down his precious pencil lead and use up so much paper, nevertheless once more, through him, the timelessness of Tristan triumphed.

Sir Tristan has spanned eight centuries. He has been re-created by artists with nothing in common except their fascination with him. Some of them have been gifted, others mediocre; some "Establishment," others rebels; some reluctant, others enthusiastic. But through this motley group he has managed to speak to the people of each age in the fashion of their day. A youth of all time, he has not been silenced by changing styles of communication or by changing means.

It is possible to picture Tristan today bursting into a home in traffic-buzzing Poitiers, the once-pastoral stronghold of Eleanor of Aquitaine, in whose twelfth-century court he was such an idol. From a television screen, he might pour out his story to a family there while also telling it, via Telstar, to you. He has, as Wagner realized, attained the perspective of the stars.

FOR FURTHER DELVING

Sir Tristan and You

If this book has been your first encounter with Sir Tristan, and if the encounter has whetted your appetite for a better acquaintance with him, here are some versions of his story, old and new, that you will enjoy reading:

Le Roman de Tristan et Iseut, Renouvelé par Joseph Bédier (Paperback, L'Edition d'Art H. Piazza, 19 Rue Bonaparte, Paris). Requires two years of French. If your French isn't that good, try *The Romance of Tristan and Iseut*, as retold by Joseph Bédier, translated by Hilaire Belloc and completed by Paul Rosenfeld (New York, Random House, Vintage Books paperback).

Tristram and Iseult, by Matthew Arnold. (In any volume of Arnold's collected poems.)

Tristram of Lyonesse, by Algernon Charles Swinburne. New York, Harper and Brothers.

Tristram, by Edwin Arlington Robinson. New York, Macmillan. Or in any volume of Robinson's collected poems.

You will enjoy listening to:

Tristan und Isolde, by Richard Wagner (recommended is the recording by *Deutsche Grammophon Gesellschaft*, made at the Bayreuth Festival, 1966, with Brigit Nilsson as Isolde, Karl Böhm conducting).

You might like to experiment with Tristan in drama, adapting one of the following to suit your circumstances:

Tristan and Isolt, by John Masefield. New York, Macmillan.

The Death of Tristram, by Laurence Binyon. In *Odes*. London, Unicorn Press.

The Famous Tragedy of the Queen of Cornwall at Tintagel in Lyonesse, by Thomas Hardy. New York, Macmillan.

There are many ways in which you can combine different approaches to Tristan, using the resources of art, literature, history, and music.

For example, parts of the Wagner opera can be used as musical background for group readings of any poet's Tristan, or as prelude or accompaniment for any dramatic production. Backdrops for plays or recitals à la troubadour can be designed in the medieval manner. Designs might be copied from the Chertsey tiles. You will find an excellent description of these, with photographs, in *Illustrations of Medieval Romance on Tiles from Chertsey Abbey*, by Roger Sherman Loomis (published by the University of Illinois, 1916). From *The Troubadours at Home, Their Lives and Personalities, Their Songs and Their World*, by Justin Smith (New York, G. P. Putnam's Sons), you can also collect graphic ideas for medieval backgrounds.

Perhaps, after reading and comparing others' versions, you may dare attempt an original Tristan including a new musical setting, perhaps written for guitar, an instrument that reproduces many of the sounds of the medieval rote.

If you travel in Europe you can still explore some of the places associated with the legend and track down traces of people connected with it. A Tristan pilgrimage might take you to:

Tintagel, Cornwall, on England's southwest coast, and the *Cunomorus stone and Castle Dor* ruins, forty miles from Tintagel. The coastal route between the two goes by Land's End, off which some geologists claim Lyonesse may once have risen. It also goes past Saint Michael's Mont, a rocky islet where folklorists believe the battle between Tristan and Morholt may have been fought. Inland lies the lovers' forest retreat.

The British Museum, London, England, to see the Chertsey Tiles.

The Breton coast in northern France. A car, camping trailer, motorbike, or bicycle trip from Dinard to Paimpol via Saint Lunaire will give you a sharp impression of the land of the other Iseut. Go out on every promontory.

Bayreuth Wagner Festival, Bayreuth, Germany. July/August, annually.

Castles of Schwangau and Hohenschwangau, Schwangau, Bavaria, in southern Germany. Ride up from Schwangau to Hohen-schwangau in a horse cart. Walk down the waterfall trail.

Poitiers, France. Here you can visit the castle of Eleanor of Aquitaine, patroness of the Tristan legend. The castle today is the Palais de Justice. In the great hall where troubadours once performed, white-wigged lawyers in black cloaks talk shop between trials. You can also enter the attached Maubergeon Tower. In the city's narrow streets outside, automobiles and people jostle each other, and university students thread through the crowds on their way to classes. Inside, only the hushed voices of lawyers remind you that you are not in the year 1170.

There are many reminders of Queen Eleanor in the parts of France she ruled. A few you might like to see are:

Her tombstone effigy on blue-and-rose plaster, along with that of her husband, Henry II, and members of the family, in the *Abbey of Fontevrault.* Also the well-ventilated abbey kitchen, which she caused to be built. Eleanor died at Fontevrault.

The heads of Eleanor and Henry topping columns in the small churches of *Belin* and *Chainier.* All the carved faces of Eleanor are strong, but the expressions differ. At Belin, she has a luscious look; in Chainier, a knowing one.

Also at Belin, ruins of the castle where Eleanor was born were a favorite playground for village children until 1928, when the owner sold the castle and its parapets were torn down for building stone. All that remains is a grass-grown-over foundation on a bluff. But in a nearby meadow at *Mons* is a chapel Eleanor ordered built. The people of the area, who have never ceased to be angry at the sale of Eleanor's castle, are proud of her chapel and keep it well. The Mayor of Belin will tell you at which farmhouse to borrow the key.

A Tristan Timetable

Here, in the order of their appearance, are the principal versions of the Tristan legend:

Earliest—exact dates unknown:	A Welsh version, by Breri, Bleddri, Bleheri, or Blehericus, and perhaps a French prose version
Probably circa 1165	Version of Chrétien de Troyes, which has perished
Circa 1170	Versions of Thomas and Eilhart von Oberg
Circa 1190–1199	Version of Béroul
1220	Version of Gottfried von Strassburg
1226	Norwegian version by Brother Robert
1230	Marie de France's *Le Lai du Chévrefeuille*
1230–1300	Proliferation. French prose. English poem. Two French poems, *Les Folies de Tristan*. Translations into Spanish, Czechoslovakian, Italian
1485	Version of Thomas Malory
1596	Inclusion in Spenser's *The Faerie Queene*
1804	Sir Walter Scott's *Sir Tristrem*
1852	Matthew Arnold's *Tristram and Iseult*
1859	Richard Wagner's opera: *Tristan und Isolde*

1871	Alfred Lord Tennyson's "The Last Tournament"
1882	Algernon Charles Swinburne's *Tristram of Lyonesse*
1904–1906	Drama and verse versions by Louis Kaufman Anspacher, Martha Austin, Josephine Carr
1917	Verse drama by Arthur Symons, *Tristan and Iseult,* dedicated to the actress, Eleanora Duse
1923	Thomas Hardy's *The Famous Tragedy of the Queen of Cornwall at Tintagel in Lyonesse*
1927	John Masefield's *Tristan and Isolt* Edwin Arlington Robinson's *Tristram*
1941	Robert Laurence Binyon's *The Death of Tristram*

Bibliography

The précis of the legend in the first chapter is a combination of the author's free translations of parts of original manuscripts, mainly from Thomas (the B. H. Wind text); some from Béroul (Muret text); a little from Eilhart (K. Wagner text); a little from Gottfried (W. Golther text); portions of *La Folie de Tristan de Berne* and *La Folie Tristan d'Oxford* (E. Hoepffner text). Also consulted was Joseph Bédier's modern version. Occasional phrases were added for transition or clarity. An effort was made to preserve the cadence, assonance, and alliteration of medieval style, while avoiding medieval dialect.

In addition to the versions of the Tristan story listed in "A Tristan Timetable" (page 183), and in addition to the sources suggested in "Sir Tristan and You" (page 179), the author's studies in the Tristan field utilized chiefly:

Ammon, Harry. "Tristan and Iseult in Medieval and Nineteenth Century Poetry," in *Georgetown University French Review*, vol. 6, no. 1 (1938).

Anglade, Joseph. "Les Troubadours et les Bretons," *Société des Langues Romans* (Montpellier), no. 29 (1929).

Anglade, Joseph. *Les Troubadours, Leurs Vies, Leurs Oeuvres, Leur Influence*. Paris: Librairie Armand Colin, 1908.

Audiau, Jean. "Les Troubadours et L'Angleterre," *Société des Lettres Sciences, Arts de la Corrèze* (1920).

Beebe, Lucius. *Edwin Arlington Robinson and the Arthurian Legend*. Privately printed. Cambridge, 1927.

Bédier, Joseph and Hazard, Paul. *Histoire de la Littérature Française*. Paris: Librairie Larousse, 1923.

Benson, Arthur Christopher. *Alfred Tennyson*. N.Y.: E. P. Dutton, 1907.

Boas, Louise Schutz. *A Great Rich Man: the Romance of Sir Walter Scott*. London: Longmans Green, 1929.

Bradbrock, M. C. *Sir Thomas Malory*. London: Longmans Green, 1958.

Brown, Rollo Walter. *Next Door to a Poet*. N.Y.: Appleton-Century-Crofts, 1937.

Buckley, Jerome Hamilton. *Tennyson: The Growth of a Poet*. Cambridge: Harvard University Press, 1960.

Carney, James. *Studies in Irish Literature and History*. Dublin Institute for Advanced Studies, 1955.

Carpenter, Frederic Ives. "Tristran the Transcendent," in *New England Quarterly* (April 1938).

Chambers, E. K. *Matthew Arnold: A Study*. London: Clarendon Press, 1947.

Cheney, Edward P. *A Short History of England*. Cambridge: Ginn, 1904.

Chesterton, G. K. and Garnett, Richard. *Tennyson*. London: Hodder and Stoughton, 1903.

Ciaramella, Michele. *A Short History of English Literature*. N.Y.: Thomas Y. Crowell, 1967.

Cohen, Gustave. *Chrétien de Troyes*. Troye: Société Académique, Académie de l'Aube, 1930.

Cronica de Origine Antiquorum Pictorum (Colbertine Ms.).

Domesday Book, Exeter Version.

Durtelle de Saint Sauveur, E. *Histoire de Bretagne*. Paris: Librairie Plon, 1935.

Elliott Binnes, L. E. *Medieval Cornwall*. London: Methuen, 1955.

Ellis, S. M. "Thomas Hardy: Some Personal Recollections," in *The Fortnightly Review*, vol. 129, N.S. 123 (January-June 1928).

Fisher, Margery. *John Masefield*, N.Y.: Walck, 1963.

Foulet, Lucien. "Marie de France et La Légende de Tristan," in *Zeitschrift für Romanische Philologie*, Halle, 1908.

Frappier, Jean. *Chrétien de Troyes: L'Homme et L'Oeuvre*. Paris: Hatier-Boivin, 1957.

Garnett, Richard. *See* Chesterton, G. K.

Gosse, Edmund. "Swinburne: Personal Recollections," in *The Fortnightly Review*, vol. LXXXV, no. 510 (June 1, 1909).

Graeme Ritchie, R. L. *Chrétien de Troyes and Scotland*. London: Clarendon Press, 1952.

Guyer, Foster Erwin. *Chrétien de Troyes: Inventor of the Modern Novel*. N.Y.: Bookman Association, 1957.

Halperin, Maurice. *Le Roman de Tristan et Iseut dans la Littérature Anglo-Américaine au xix et xx Siècles*. Paris: Jouve, 1931.

Hardy, Florence Emily. *The Life of Thomas Hardy*. N.Y.: St. Martin's, 1962.

Hare, Humphrey. *Swinburne: A Biographical Approach*. London: Chatto and Windus, 1949.

Hazard, Paul. *See* Bédier, Joseph.

Hébert, Marcel. *Tétrologie, Tristan et Iseult, Parsifal de R. Wagner*. Paris: Genier, 1894.

Henderson, Charles. *Essays in Cornish History*. London: Clarendon Press, 1935.

Hutton, Richard H. *Sir Walter Scott*. London: Macmillan, 1878.

Istel, Edgard. "How Wagner Worked," in *Musical Quarterly* (January 1933).

Jackson, John P. *The Bayreuth of Wagner*. N.Y.: Lovell, 1891.

Jeanroy, A. *La Première Génération des Troubadours*, in *Romania*, vol. LVI. Paris, 1930.

Jenner, Henry. *The Irish Immigrations into Cornwall*. Royal Cornwall Polytechnic Society, 1917.

Johnson, E. D. H. *The Alien Vision of Victorian Poetry*. Princeton: Princeton University Press, 1952.

Kelly, Amy. *Eleanor of Aquitaine and the Four Kings*. Cambridge: Harvard University Press, 1950.

Kerr, John Edward, Jr. "The Character of Marc in Myth and Legend," in *Modern Language Notes*, vol. X, no. 1 (January 1894).

Kolb, Annette. *Le Roi Louis de Bavière et Richard Wagner*. Paris: Albin Michel, 1947.

Leith, Mrs. Disney. *The Boyhood of Algernon Charles Swinburne*. London: Chatto and Windus, 1917.

Leroy, Maxime. "Autour de Tristan et Iseult, d'après une correspondence inédite de Wagner," in *La Revue Blanche*.

Loomis, Gertrude Schoepperle. *Tristan and Isolt: A Study of the Sources of the Romance*. N.Y.: Burt Franklin, 1963.

Loomis, Roger Sherman. "Bleheris and the Tristan Story," in *Modern Language Notes*, vol. X, no. 1 (January 1894).

Longford, Elizabeth. *Queen Victoria*. N.Y.: Harper and Row, 1964.

Maule, Henry. *History of the Picts*. Edinburgh, 1756. Published by Robert Freebairn and Sold in His Shop in the Parliament-Close.

Meray, Antony. *La Vie au Temps de Trouvères*. Paris: A. Claudin, 1873.

Nennius. *Historia Britonum*.

Panofsky, Walter. *Wieland Wagner*. Bremen: Schuman, 1964.

Paul, Herbert. *Matthew Arnold*. London: Macmillan, 1902.

Reisiger, Hans. *The Restless Star*. N.Y.: Century, 1932.

Rougemont, Denis de. *Love in the Western World*. N.Y.: Harcourt, Brace, 1940.

Roujoux, M. de. *Histoire des Rois et des Ducs de Bretagne.* Paris: Dufey, 1839.

Scott, Archibald B. *The Pictish Nation: Its People and Its Church.* Edinburgh and London: T. N. Foulis, 1918.

Scott, Sir Walter. *Narrative of the Life of Sir Walter Scott, Bart.* Begun by Himself and continued by J. O. Lockhart and J. M. Deni. N.Y.: E. P. Dutton, 1906.

Skelton, Geoffrey. *Wagner at Bayreuth: Experiment and Tradition.* London: Barrie and Rockliff, 1965.

Tacitus. *Agricola.*

Wagner, Kurt, ed. *Eilhart von Oberg Tristant: I. Die alten Bruchstücke.* Bonn and Leipzig: Kurt Schroeder, 1924.

Weston, Jessie L. *The Legends of the Wagner Drama.* London: Longmans Green, 1903.

Williams, Mary. *More About Bleddri.* Paris: Etudes Celtiques, Librairie Dioz, 1937.

Guide to Pronunciation

Note: Italics indicate accent. As far as possible, a modern pronunciation is given for the archaic French. An *n* following an *h* usually conveys resonance and is often, though not always, silent. (It should be understood that such phonetic pronunciations can only approximate non-English sounds.)

l'amant	lah-*mahn*
l'amour courtois	lah-*moor* kur-*twah*
l'amoureux	lah-moor-*uh*
Andret	*ahn*-dray
Bayreuth	by-*royt*

la beale Isoud	lah beel ee-*sood*
Blanchefleur	*blansh*-fler
Bleheri	*blay*-air-ee
Blehericus	bleh-*hair*-ee-cus
Brangäne	brahn-*gay*-nuh
Brangien	*brahn*-zhee-*en*
broch	broke
Cliges	kleezh
Denoalen	deh-*no*-ahl-en
Drust	drewst
Drystan	dri-*stan*
Festspielhaus	*fest*-shpeel-hows
Frocin	*froh*-sahn (flat *a*)
Gondoine	gohn-*dwahn*
Gorvenal	gor-ven-*ahl*
Guenelon	gwen-eh-lohn
Guillaume	gee-*yohm*
Hoël	hoh-*el*
Hohenschwangau	hoh-en-*shvahn*-gow
Husdent	oos-*dahn*
Iseut	ee-*suht*
Isolde	ee-*zold*-uh
Issoire	ee-*swahr*
jongleur	zhon-*glur*
Kaherdin	kah-hair-*dan* (short *a*)
Kurwenal	*koor*-veh-*nal*
Liebestrank	*lee*-bis-tronk
Loone	*loo*-nuh
Ludwig	*lyoud*-vish
Mabinogien	mah-bin-*oh*-gee-en
Marke	*mark*-uh

Maubergeon	moh-bair-zhay-*ohn*
Maubergeonne, La	moh-bair-zhay-*onn*, lah
Melot	*may*-lot
minnesänger	*min*-nuh-*zeng*-uh
Morte d'Arthur	mort dar-*tyur*
Morholt	mor-*holt*
Morois	Moh-*rwah*
Neuschwanstein	noy-*shvahn*-stine
Ogrin	oh-*grahn* (flat *a*)
Poitiers	pwah-*tyay*
Poitou	pwah-*too*
Riol	ree-*ohl*
Rivalen	ree-vah-len
romans courtois	roh-manh coor-*twah*
soupirant	soo-peer-*ahn*
Strauss, Richard Georg	strows, *ree*-card *gay*-org
suppliant	syou-plee-*ahn*
Thomas	toe-*mah*
Tintagel	tin-*tah*-jel
Todestrank	*toe*-dis-tronk
Triscan	*tree*-scahn
Tristan	*tree*-stahn
triste	treest
Tristrant	tree-*strahnt*
Troyes, Chrétien de	*trwah*, *cray*-tee-ahn (flat a) duh
von Oberg, Eilhart	fon *oh*-bairg, *eyl*-hart
Wagner, Richard	*vahg*-nair, *ree*-card
Wesendonk, Mathilde	*vay*-sayn-donk, mah-til-day
Wieland	*vee*-lahnt

Index